✳ The Mystery and Magic Series ✳

Gods
and
Goddesses

Robert Ingpen & Molly Perham

CHELSEA HOUSE PUBLISHERS

First published in the United States
by Chelsea House Publishers, 1996

Editor Diana Briscoe
Designer Megra Mitchell
Design Assistants Karen Ferguson,
Victoria Furbisher
Art Director John Strange
Editorial Director Pippa Rubinstein

ISBN 0–7910–3927–7

Typeset by Dragon's World Ltd in Caslon, Century Old Style and Helvetica.
Printed in Italy

✳ Contents ✳

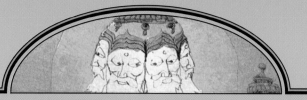

❋ Contents ❋

✳ Introduction ✳

The great nations of ancient times worshipped more than one god. Most believed there were a number of gods and goddesses, each of whom was responsible for a different element of nature such as the sun, the sky, the wind, or the rain. Others were in charge of concepts like love, revenge, wisdom or the arts. These immortals were all-powerful and could do great good or great harm. People sacrificed to them so that they would send good weather, make the crops grow, send favourable winds for sailors, or give victory in war.

Gods and goddesses were thought of as people, and were often arranged together as families.

In ancient Greece Zeus, god of the sky and the weather, was king of the divine family. In Norse legends, Odin is All-Father of gods and men. In the sacred books of the Hindus, Brahma is the supreme god, creator of the universe and the father god of the trinity.

Although they were supposed to be very wise, many gods had the same failings as humans. They quarrelled with one another; sometimes they cheated men or each other, and often interfered in human affairs. Stories of gods, goddesses and the mysteries of creation are told in traditional legends all around the world.

Molly Perham

Mesopotamia

The ancient myths of Mesopotamia (modern Syria and Iraq) show that the Sumerian and Akkadian people believed in a large number of deities, of greater and lesser importance. Some were responsible for the elements; others were patrons of the various cities and states.

One of the most widely known myths tells of the flood which was sent by four of the great gods – Anu, Enlil, Ninurta and Innana – to destroy life on earth. But a fifth god, Enki, revealed the secret plan to a man called Ut-Napishtim and told him to build a boat in order to be saved. The Sumerians often had different names for their gods than those used by the Akkadians.

Anu was the father, or king, of the gods, and also the god of the sky. He was the son of Anshar and

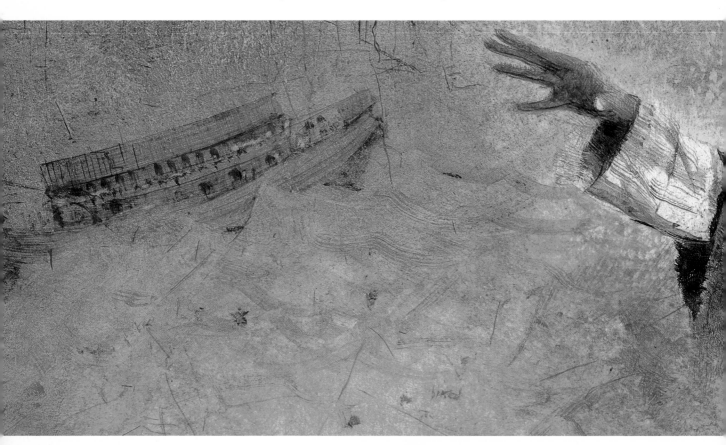

Kishar, and father of Enki. These are all described as great gods, because they were the first descendants of the primeval Apsu, the mass of fresh water beneath the earth, and Tiamat, the mass of sea water around the earth.

Marduk was the patron god of Babylon. One myth tells how he destroyed Tiamat and created the universe from her body.

Enlil, the counsellor of the gods, was also the god of winds, storm and rain. He made the whole earth rich and prosperous. He made the pickaxe, so that men could till the soil and build houses. He also created two lesser gods – Emesh (summer) and Enten (winter) – to provide the land with plants and animals and make it fertile. Ninurta was Enlil's son and the club-wielding champion of the gods.

Enki was the god of water and wisdom. He was known to the Akkadians as Ea. Enki sent the Seven Sages to teach the arts and skills of civilization to mankind. In some myths he and his wife Ninhursag, goddess of the earth, were responsible for the creation of gods and humans, and for the organization of the world.

Nergal was the god who brought about mass destruction by war or by the plague. One of the ancient myths describes how he took over the underworld by dethroning its queen, Ereshkigal. He spared her life only when she invited him to marry her and take over her realm.

Innana, the goddess of fertility and love, and also a warrior goddess, was known to the Akkadians as Ishtar. The story of Innana's descent to the underworld is another of the best known Mesopotamian myths.

▽ The civilization of Mesopotamia grew in the lands that lie between the rivers Tigris and Euphrates. Both rivers were subject to frequent, disastrous floods – which probably accounts for this ancient myth.

The Descent of Innana

Innana, the beautiful goddess of love, decided to descend to the underworld of Kurnugi, which was ruled by her sister Ereshkigal. She was as ugly as Innana was beautiful.

When she arrived at the gate of Kurnugi, Innana said to the gate-keeper, 'Open the gate for me to come in. Open it at once or I will smash it down.'

The gate-keeper begged her to wait while he went to speak to his mistress. Ereshkigal was furious when she learned of Innana's arrogant behaviour. 'What does she want with me?' she snarled. 'All right, let her in, but treat her according to the ancient rites.'

So the gate-keeper allowed the goddess through the first gate, but removed her crown. Then he let her in through the second gate, but took away the rings in her ears. At the third gate her necklace was removed; at the fourth gate the amulet from her breast; at the fifth gate the girdle from her waist; and at the sixth gate the bangles from her wrists and ankles.

Finally, at the seventh gate, the gate-keeper stripped off her clothes, so that by the time Innana was brought before Ereshkigal she was completely naked and helpless, for all her power had been lost with her clothes and her regalia.

Ereshkigal called her vizier Namtar and said, 'Take Innana and imprison her. And let loose the sixty diseases to attack her eyes, her arms, her feet, her heart, and every other part of her body.'

As a result of Innana's imprisonment the earth lost its fertility. Plants wilted and animals and humans refused to mate and produce new offspring. Eventually the great god Enki was asked to intercede. He created a beautiful young man and sent him to Kurnugi to charm Ereshkigal and persuade her to release Innana.

When the young man asked for a drink from the skin containing the water of life, she cursed him. However, Ereshkigal accepted him as a substitute for Innana, and the fertility goddess was set free.

As Innana returned through the seven gates her clothes and jewellery were given back to her, and with her freedom everything on earth returned to normal.

Gods and Goddesses of Egypt

The ancient Egyptians worshipped many different gods and goddesses. Some of these immortals had human form; others had the heads of birds or animals.

Each Egyptian city had its own pantheon, or collection, of gods. The priests of these cities rivalled each other to prove that their own god and his entourage of deities had created the universe. The gods of Heliopolis in the delta of the river Nile became the most important.

RA-ATUM

▷▷ Ra-Atum represented the evening sun who had to return to the womb of Nut to be renewed each night.

Worship of the sun god Ra originated at Heliopolis. Ra had a falcon's head and a sacred eye with which he destroyed his enemies. He travelled across the heavens in a boat known as Millions of Years.

Each morning, having overcome the powers of darkness, Ra started out in the east. Throughout the day his glorious presence shed light and heat down onto the earth.

At sunset Ra disappeared into the underworld in the west. His boat sailed along the river of death, taking with it the souls of those who had died during the day.

In time Ra became identified with the god Atum, the original creator of Heliopolis. Atum emerged from the waters on to a primeval island and created Shu, god of the air, and Tefnut, goddess of moisture. These two produced Geb, the earth god, and Nut, the sky goddess. From their union came Osiris and Seth, and their sisters Isis and Nephthys.

ISIS

Isis, symbol of divine motherhood, was married to Osiris and was also his sister. She was regarded as the ideal woman, wife and mother.

Isis and Osiris had a son called

Horus, who was identified with the ruling pharaoh and was often represented by a falcon.

OSIRIS

The ancient Egyptians believed that there was life after death. The afterworld was divided into twelve divisions, like the twelve hours of the night, and in the sixth sat Osiris, the judge of the dead. Osiris was attended by various deities. Thoth, the god of wisdom and learning, presided over a large pair of scales, while Ma'at, the goddess of justice, and Anubis, god of embalming, were present to ensure that the proceedings were carried out fairly.

The heart of the dead man was placed by Anubis on one side of the pair of scales. A feather, the symbol of Ma'at, was put on the other side. If the heart balanced equally with the feather, the dead man could pass into the blessed afterlife in Osiris's underworld. If the heart weighed too heavy, it was thrown to terrible monsters.

HATHOR

Hathor was the goddess of joy and love, of the sky, and of the west – the abode of the dead. She appeared in the form of a cow, with a head-dress made up of two plumes and a solar disc. Her body was decorated with stars symbolizing her role as a sky goddess.

APIS

At Memphis a bull called Apis was worshipped by the Egyptians. The animal chosen for this role had to be black, with a white square on his forehead and another mark that looked like an eagle on his back. Under his tongue there was a lump in the shape of a sacred scarab, or beetle.

As soon as a young bull with these markings was found, he was put into a building facing the east and fed with milk for four months. Then, at full moon, the priests put the animal into a magnificently decorated boat and conveyed him down the River Nile to Memphis.

Apis the Bull had a temple, with two chapels and a court for exercise. He was tended by priests, and sacrifices were made to him. Once every year, about the time when the Nile began to rise before the annual flood, a golden cup was thrown into the river, and a grand festival was held to celebrate the bull's birthday. The Egyptians believed that during this festival the crocodiles forgot their natural ferocity and became harmless.

◁◁ After Isis restored Osiris's body, he could have returned to the world of the living. However, he chose to remain in the world of the dead and so became Khenti-Amentiu, First of the Westerners and King of the Dead. Appointed as judge of the underworld by Ra, he had authority over anyone, god or mortal, who came before his throne.

The Death of Osiris

In Heliopolis, Osiris, Isis, Seth and Nephthys were all the children of Geb, the earth god, and Nut, the sky goddess. Osiris was married to Isis, and Seth to Nephthys. Osiris was a good and wise god, who as king of the Egyptians brought them knowledge of agriculture and the arts. Seth became very jealous of his brother's popularity, and plotted to kill him.

Osiris made the valley of the Nile into a civilized country. He gave the people laws, government, the institution of marriage, and taught them how to worship the gods. Then he set out to conquer the rest of the world. While he was away Seth gathered about him seventy-two conspirators and prepared a huge banquet to celebrate his brother's return.

At the banquet Seth produced a beautiful chest made of precious wood and promised to give it to any guest who fitted exactly inside. Several guests lay down in the chest, but they were either too small or too large in size. When Osiris took his turn, he fitted the chest perfectly, for Seth had designed the chest for this purpose. As soon as Osiris was inside, Seth and his companions closed and sealed the lid and flung the chest into the Nile.

When Isis heard what had happened she was distraught with grief. Cutting off her hair and dressing herself in black clothes, she set off in search of her husband's body, aided by the god Anubis. For some time they searched in vain, for the chest had been carried many miles by the waves. It was finally washed up on the shores of Byblos on the Phoenician coast, where it became entangled in the reeds that grew at the edge of the water.

The divine power in Osiris's body imparted such strength to the reeds that they grew into a huge tree, enclosing the coffin in the trunk. The tree was eventually felled and erected as a column in the palace of the king of Phoenicia.

At last, with the help of Anubis, Isis discovered what had happened. She went to the royal palace and offered her services as a servant. Once inside, she threw off her disguise and appeared as a goddess, surrounded with thunder and lightning. Striking the column with her sacred wand, Isis caused it to split open and give up her husband's coffin.

Isis hid the coffin in the depths of the forest, but

◁ Seth was sometimes described as having red hair and at other times was shown with the head of an animal that looked something like an aardvark.

He often took on the form of a hippopotamus – an animal much feared by the Egyptians because it would attack boats that got too close to it.

Seth discovered it. He cut Osiris's body into fourteen pieces and scattered them throughout Egypt. After a long search Isis managed to find thirteen pieces, the fishes of the Nile having eaten the last. This she replaced with an imitation of sycamore wood. She buried her husband's body at Philoe, which from that time on became a place of pilgrimage. A magnificent temple was erected in honour of Osiris, and at every place where one of his limbs had been found other temples were built to commemorate the event.

Meanwhile Horus had grown to manhood and was determined to avenge his father's death. In a vicious and bloody fight, Seth pulled out one of his nephew's eyes, but Horus was finally the victor. A tribunal of judges met in the Great Hall of Judgement to decide how the kingdom should be divided.

Thoth decided that Horus should succeed his father on the throne as a living king, and his plucked out eye was restored to him. Osiris became king and judge of the dead in the underworld. His soul was supposed always to inhabit the body of the bull Apis, and at his death to transfer itself to his successor. Seth was disgraced for eternity. Good had triumphed over Evil.

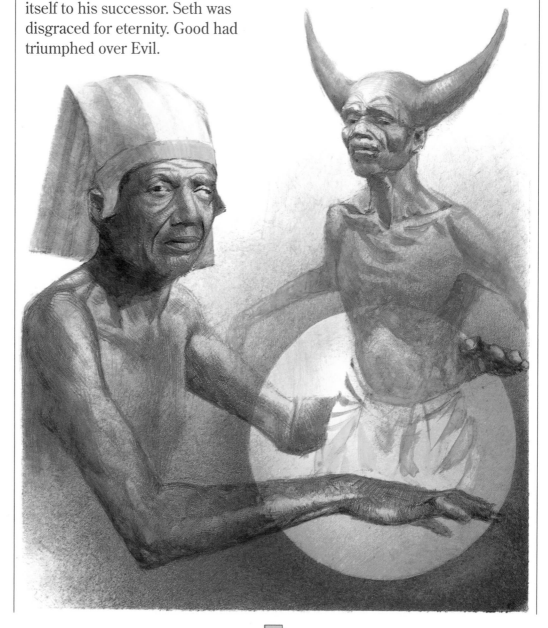

Gods and Goddesses of India

The sacred books of the Hindus are called the *Vedas*. These are a collection of stories which set out the religious ideas of the Arya, a people who invaded India from the northwest in about 1500 BC. The Aryans spoke Sanskrit, a language very similar to that of the ancient Greeks, and some of the stories resemble the Greek myths.

▽ Brahma is usually shown with four bearded heads facing in different directions.

His wife was Sarasvati, the goddess of wisdom and patroness of the arts. She is said to have invented Sanskrit, the language of the Hindu scriptures. She is worshipped by Indian students and schoolchildren, who will offer her a pen or pencil before the start of a difficult class.

BRAHMA

The supreme god of the Hindus is Brahma. He is the creator of the universe and the father god of the trinity, three gods in one. The other two members of the Hindu trinity are Vishnu the preserver and Shiva the destroyer, who are constantly warring against each other.

Brahma, Vishnu and Shiva therefore stand for the three processes of creation, preservation and destruction that are continually going on in the universe.

SHIVA

Shiva the Destroyer stands for the forces of nature, but in spite of his name he represents the forces that create life as well as those that destroy it.

Shiva appears as a dancing figure with four arms, which are symbols of his unceasing activities. He is also sometimes known as Nataraja, Lord of the Dance. His wife Parvati also changes her form and is represented in many different ways.

GANESHA

from the path of those who worship him correctly, but places them in the way of humans who do not pay due homage to the gods. He is often called on by people who are about to start up a new business, move to a new house or go on a journey.

SKANDA

Shiva's other son is the six-headed warrior god, Skanda, who carries a spear and rides on a peacock.

As soon as Skanda was born, he terrified the other gods by shattering the mountains with his arrows. They begged Indra, the storm god, to get rid of him. Indra hurled a thunderbolt at Skanda which split the warrior god's side. But instead of killing him, another warrior came out of his body.

This god of scribes and merchants is the son of Shiva. Parvati wanted to have a child, but Shiva did not want to become involved in family life. He told her to make a child from a piece of red cloth. She did so, and the cloth became a handsome young son.

However when Shiva touched the boy's head, it fell off, so it was replaced with the head of an elephant belonging to Indra, the god of storms.

▽ Another story says that Shiva once looked into a lake, from which emerged six children. These were looked after by his wife, Parvati, She loved them so much and hugged them so hard that they were all squeezed into one body – although the six heads remained.

Skanda is also called Karttikeya and Kumara and he leads the army of the gods into battle.

Ganesha is also known as the Lord of Obstacles. He removes them

VISHNU

Vishnu is the god who preserves life. He is reborn on earth from time to time to help and educate mankind. Each time he descends in a different form. These descents are called avatars.

Vishnu's first avatar was a fish called Matsya. The fish instructed the sage Manu to build a boat and take with him on board seeds of all created things. In this way Vishnu saved life on earth from destruction by the great flood.

The second avatar was in the form of a tortoise called Kurma. The gods were churning the ocean in order to obtain the elixir of immortality. The churning-pole was a mountain that rested on the bottom of the ocean, and the great snake Vasuki was used as a rope to turn it. Vishnu transformed himself into a tortoise and took the pole on his back to protect the earth from the violence of the churning.

In his third avatar Vishnu transformed himself into a huge boar, Varaha. The earth had been dragged down to the bottom of the ocean by a powerful demon. Varaha lifted it up with his tusks and saved it from drowning.

In his fourth avatar Vishnu became Narasimha, a man-lion. A good demon called Prahlada, who worshipped Vishnu, was challenged by his father to prove the existence of his god. Vishnu descended as a

MATSYA

KURMA

VARAHA   NARASIMHA   VAMANA

man-lion and disembowelled the wicked demon.

The fifth avatar was as the dwarf Vamana. The gods asked the demons who controlled the earth for a share in it – as much as the dwarf could step over in three strides. Vamana strode across the heaven, the earth and the atmosphere in his three strides, and so won all of them for the gods.

The sixth avatar was called Parashurama, who destroyed all the warriors and gave the earth to the priests to rule.

The seventh avatar was Prince Rama, a brave and virtuous hero who won the beautiful Sita for his wife by bending and stringing a huge bow. When Sita was carried off by a demon king named Ravana, Rama rescued her with the help of Hanuman, god-chief of the monkey people. Hanuman was the son of Parvana, the god of the winds.

The eighth avatar was Krishna, a royal prince renowned for his flute-playing, who had been brought up as a cowherd. Krishna saved the earth by killing the serpent Kaliya.

The ninth avatar was Buddha, a form taken by Vishnu to induce the Asuras, opponents of the gods, to abandon the teachings of the Vedas, so that they lost their strength and supremacy.

Kalki is the name of the tenth and final avatar, in which Vishnu will appear at the end of the present age of the world, riding on a white horse to destroy all evil and wickedness, and restore humanity to virtue and purity.

Ancient Greece

The ancient Greek gods and goddesses looked like men and women, except that they were taller, stronger, wiser and more beautiful. They were not spirits, but they could not be seen by mortals unless they wanted to show themselves – and then it was often not in their true forms. These immortals lived on Mt Olympus in Thessaly. They lived for ever because they ate special food called ambrosia and drank nectar.

ZEUS

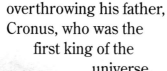

Zeus was the king of the Greek gods. According to legend, he became the supreme god of Olympus by overthrowing his father, Cronus, who was the first king of the universe.

Cronus knew that he would one day be turned off the throne by one of his own children, and to try to prevent this he swallowed each one as soon as it was born. The baby Zeus was saved by his mother, Rhea, and brought up in a cave on Mount Ida in Crete. When Zeus reached manhood he forced his father to cough up the children he had swallowed, and together they conquered Cronus and took over the world. Zeus took the heavens, Poseidon took the oceans, and Pluto became god of the underworld.

Zeus first married the goddess Metis, with whom he had a daughter, Athene. He then married his sister Hera, and their children were Hebe, Eileithyia and Ares, the god of war. However, Zeus loved many other women besides Hera, and also fathered Apollo, Artemis, Hermes, Perseus, Dionysus, Persephone and Herakles.

▷ Poseidon was particularly feared by seafarers. If any sailor crossed him, or did not worship the god as required, then he would fly into a rage and send storms and violent weather.

POSEIDON

This powerful Lord of the Oceans lived in a golden palace at the bottom of the sea. From time to time he rode out over the waves in a chariot drawn by sea horses. He carried a three-pronged spear called a trident and was accompanied by mermen, called tritons, who blew shrill blasts on conch shells to warn everyone to keep out of the way.

Poseidon was also the god of storms and earthquakes, the creator of horses and the patron of horse races and bull dancing.

On one occasion he contested with the goddess Athene who could produce the gift most useful to mortals. Athene produced the olive, while Poseidon produced a horse. The gods judged that the olive was the more useful of the two and gave the city of Athens, from which it takes its name, to Athene.

The sea god was married to the sea nymph Amphitrite, and their son, Triton, was also a merman. When Poseidon made advances to another nymph called Scylla, Amphitrite used magic to turn her rival into a dog-headed monster. He was also father to Charybdis, a sea monster who attacked ships.

Pluto and Persephone

Pluto was the Greek god of the underworld and the dead. He was also known as Hades, and his underground kingdom was called the House of Hades. Pluto was a stern ruler who listened to neither flattery nor prayers. Where he was worshipped no temples were built in his honour, and only black bulls were offered to him as sacrifice. He very seldom allowed any of his subjects to leave Hades – although he was once persuaded by the marvellous music of Orpheus to allow Orpheus's wife, Eurydice, to return to earth.

Pluto wore a helmet that made him invisible and rode in a carriage drawn by four black horses. On an excursion to earth he was struck by one of Eros's arrows. Just at that moment he was driving through a meadow where Persephone, the daughter of the earth mother Demeter, was picking flowers. Pluto fell in love with Persephone instantly and carried her off by force to his kingdom, where he made her his queen.

Demeter was grief-stricken, and wandered all over the world looking for her child. Eventually she put a curse on the land, so that cattle died and seed failed to sprout. Then she went to Zeus and told him she would only remove the curse if he ordered Pluto to release Persephone. Zeus agreed, on condition that Persephone had not eaten any food during her stay in the underworld. Otherwise, the Fates forbade her release.

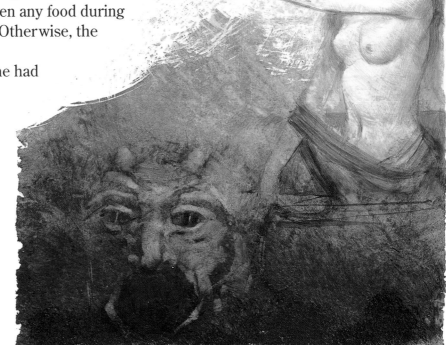

Unfortunately, Persephone had eaten six seeds from a pomegranate. When she was told of Zeus's decision, she burst into tears. Pluto, seeing his beloved wife so sad, begged Zeus to relent.

And so it was arranged that Persephone, like the seed of the corn, should spend six months of each year under the ground with her husband and six months on the earth's surface with her mother.

APOLLO

A pollo, son of Zeus by Leto, was one of the greatest Greek gods. He had all the qualities that the ancient Greeks admired most: he was strong and beautiful, wise and just. When Apollo was little more than a baby he slew the great dragon Python which guarded the oracle at Delphi.

Apollo was worshipped all over Greece and people went to the oracle at Delphi to ask for advice. He was the god of many different things – of light, intellect, the arts, medicine, music and prophecy.

He was also an archer, and usually carried a bow as well as a lyre.

The lyre was invented by his half-brother, Hermes. The crafty Hermes stole a herd of cattle that belonged to Apollo. When the theft was discovered, Zeus ordered Hermes to return the cattle. But Apollo was so delighted when he heard Hermes play the lyre, which he had invented, that he let Hermes keep the cattle in exchange for it.

Apollo was once struck by one of Eros's arrows and fell in love with a forest nymph called Daphne. Unfortunately for him, Daphne had been struck by another arrow that repelled love. When Apollo pursued Daphne, she prayed to her father, who was a river god, to help. He turned her into a laurel bush, which thus became sacred to Apollo in memory of his lost Daphne.

▷ The custom of giving laurel wreathes to the winners of sport events and artistic competitions has come down to us from ancient Greece. The victors of the ancient Olympic Games were honoured with a laurel wreath.

ARTEMIS

Artemis the huntress was the twin sister of Apollo. The divine twins were the only children of Leto by Zeus. When Niobe, who had also been loved by Zeus, rashly boasted that she was much more fortunate than Leto because she had seven sons and seven daughters, Leto summoned her children to punish Niobe. Artemis shot the seven girls and Apollo the seven boys.

Artemis was the goddess of the moon, of hunting, and of the open countryside. Artemis was kind to all young things, including human babies and their mothers, who prayed to her when their children were being born. However, Artemis did not want love and marriage for herself, and the nymphs who attended her had to promise to remain unmarried. When one of them, Callisto, allowed herself to be seduced by Zeus, Artemis would not listen to her excuses. Zeus tried to protect Callisto by changing her into a bear, but Artemis tracked her down and killed her with an arrow.

Another of her victims was Actaeon, a youth who came across Artemis and her nymphs bathing in a forest pool. The goddess was so angry that she turned him into a stag. He was chased and torn to pieces by his own hounds.

Even Agamemnon, king of Mycenae, suffered from Artemis's anger when he killed a sacred stag. She took her revenge by inflicting his army with the plague and becalming his ships in port when they were about to sail to Troy.

ATHENE

Athene, the daughter of Zeus by Metis, the goddess of wisdom, sprang from her father's head fully grown and wearing armour. She was both the protector of brave warriors and the goddess of wisdom and knowledge.

As the goddess of wisdom she presided over all kinds of skills – both those of men, such as agriculture and navigation, and those of women, such as spinning, weaving and needlework. She invented the flute, plough, chariot, horse bridle and the ship among many other useful things.

She was particularly fond of heroes and heroines who undertook difficult quests. It was thanks to her advice and assistance that Perseus, the son of Danaë and Zeus, managed to kill the dreadful gorgon, Medusa, whose glance turned men to stone.

Although Athene was as modest as Artemis, she was far more merciful than her half-sister. When Teiresias accidentally caught sight of her while she was bathing, she blinded him, but she also gave him the gift of prophecy. He became the most famous seer in all of Greece because he could understand the languages of the birds.

She was a great peacemaker, and would always rather settle a dispute by arbitration than by use of arms. In criminal trials in Athens, if the judges were equally divided as to the guilt or innocence of the accused, Athene's vote was always cast on the side of mercy.

How Arachne challenged Athene

A rachne was a princess of Colophon in Lydia, a city renowned for its excellent weavers and purple dyes. As a young girl Arachne was very skilled at spinning sheep's wool into thread and weaving beautiful tapestries. She was so proud of her talent that she challenged Athene to a competition.

Athene was confident that a mere mortal could never be compared with a goddess and offered Arachne the chance to withdraw her challenge. Arachne refused, and so the contest proceeded. Each took her place at the loom and attached the web to the beam. Then they passed the slender shuttle in and out among the threads. Both worked with lightning speed, their skilful hands so rapid that onlookers scarcely saw them move.

Athene wove on her web a scene of her contest with Neptune, ruler of the sea. In each corner were pictures illustrating the displeasure of the gods at presumptuous mortals who dared to challenge them. These were warnings to her rival to give up the contest before it was too late.

Arachne filled her web with designs chosen to show the love affairs of the gods. One scene showed Europa deceived by Zeus in the disguise of a bull. Encouraged by the tameness of the animal, Europa had got on his back, and the bull-Zeus was swimming out to sea. The weaving was wonderfully well done, and so realistic, you would have thought it was a real bull and real water in which it swam.

Athene studied the beautiful tapestry made by Arachne, her anger growing as she failed to find any imperfection. She struck furiously at the web with her shuttle and tore it in pieces. Then she turned Arachne into a spider and suspended her from a thread. And so Arachne's fate for daring to challenge a goddess was to spin and weave for ever with thread drawn from her own body.

APHRODITE

Aphrodite, daughter of Zeus, rose out of the sea and stepped on to land from a sea shell. She was therefore worshipped as the goddess of calm seas and prosperous voyages, but more importantly as the goddess of love and beauty. She was more beautiful than any other goddess, and her power was so great that she could bewitch mortal men and even the gods themselves.

▷ Aphrodite had several children as a result of her numerous love affairs. Among them were the mortal Aeneas of Troy, and the gods Priapus and Hermaphrodite.

Eros was Aphrodite's son by Ares, the god of war. One day, while playing with Eros, Aphrodite was wounded by one of his arrows and thus she fell in love with a very handsome youth called Adonis.

One day a wild boar killed Adonis, and Aphrodite was so upset that Zeus allowed him to come back to earth for six months of every year, and spend the other six months in the underworld. While he was in the underworld, there were no leaves and flowers; but when he returned to earth, plants and trees started to grow again.

EROS

Eros, the god of physical love, was the youngest of the Olympian gods. Romans called him Cupid. He flew around shooting people with his little bow. Some of his arrows were tipped with gold, and some with lead. People who were shot with golden arrows instantly fell in love. The lead arrows made unsuitable couples dislike each other.

Unfortunately Eros had a very mischievous nature and sometimes used the arrows unwisely. Golden arrows might be shot into the hearts of those who were quite unsuited to each other. Even worse, Eros would shoot a golden arrow into a would-be lover and a leaden one into the woman he desired.

ARES

The Greek god of war was called Ares. The Romans called their god of war Mars, and this is the name that is best known now. Unlike the

Romans, the Greeks were never very keen on war, so Ares was not a very popular god. Ares fell in love with Aphrodite, the goddess of love and beauty, and Eros was their son.

AEOLUS

The son of Poseidon by a mortal woman, Aeolus was the god of the winds. He became a sea captain and, when he realized that ships could be blown along by the winds instead of having to depend on oars, he invented sails. Married to Aurora, goddess of the dawn, they had six sons who each looked after a wind.

Aeolus gave Odysseus. the Greek hero, a leather bag containing all the winds that might harm his ship on the way home. But his crew were so curious that they opened the bag and let the winds escape, so that the voyage became a disaster.

Gods and Goddesses of Asgard

The Norsemen of Scandinavia thought of their gods as large human beings, who ate, slept, were born and died, and could be overcome in battle. Tales of their exploits are contained in two collections of Icelandic legends called *Eddas*. There were two families of gods: the Aesir, who included Odin and Thor; and the Vanir, who were closely connected with the dead.

ODIN

According to Norse mythology, in the beginning, Odin and his two brothers Vili and Ve slew the giant Ymir and formed the universe out of his body. Odin then created day and night, and set the sun and moon in the heavens. He made man out of the branch of an ash tree and woman out of an elm.

Odin was the chief of the Aesir gods. He was extremely wise, but had only one eye, for he had sacrificed the other as the price of a drink from the god Mimir's well of wisdom. On Odin's shoulders perched two ravens, Thought and Memory. These ravens flew round the world every day and told Odin what was happening. At his feet crouched two wolves. When he went to war, Odin rode his eight-footed horse Sleipnir and carried his all-powerful sword. He wore an eagle helmet and a magic ring.

Odin was married to Frigga, goddess of the earth, but he also loved other goddesses and mortal women. Of his many sons Thor, god of thunder, was the most powerful.

VALKYRIES

These magnificent young women were the warrior handmaidens of Odin. They rode into battle on great war horses and selected the most heroic warriors who had died, to enter Valhalla. They also waited on these warriors as they feasted with Odin.

ASGARD

Asgard was the mysterious heavenly abode of the Aesir gods. It looked fairly

similar to the homes of the Vikings down in Midgard (our Earth).

At the centre was a great hall called Valhalla, where Odin sat on his golden throne and received the spirits of warriors slain in battle. Asgard was linked to Midgard by a rainbow bridge known as Bifrost. The icy region of Jotunheim was the home of the frost giants.

HEIMDALL

Heimdall was the watchman of the gods. He stood guard on the rainbow bridge, Bifrost, to prevent the giants from forcing their way over. Heimdall required very little sleep and could see by night as well as by day. His ears were so acute that he could even hear the grass grow. No sound escaped him.

▽ Heimdall always carried a great horn, called the Gjallarhorn, so that he could alert the gods and goddesses of Asgard to the start of the last battle against the giants and other monsters. This battle was to be called Ragnarok (or Doom). In some legends he is said to be the father of all humans.

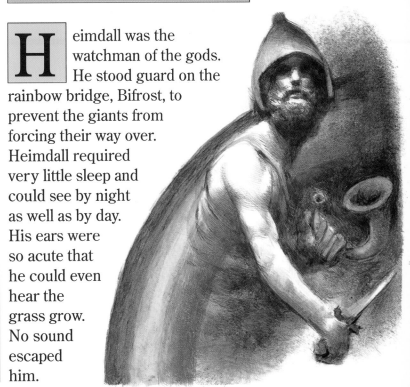

Loki, God of Mischief

A handsome young fire demon called Loki was so charming to the gods that he was made one of the Aesir. Loki was the son of a giant and had the magical powers to fly and change his shape. He was the father of three monstrous children – an enormous wolf called Fenris, the Midgard Serpent which lay coiled around the Earth, and Hel, queen of the underworld.

When the gods made Asgard their home, a giant offered to build a wall round it to keep out their enemies. It was agreed that if the giant finished the wall before the end of winter, he could have the sun, the moon and Freya, the beautiful goddess of love, as a reward. The gods made this bargain thinking that the giant would never finish on time.

On Loki's advice, the gods allowed the giant to use his horse to help him. But to their dismay, it turned out to be a magic horse that hauled the huge stones at great speed. The gods, fearing that they would lose Freya and the sun and moon as well, blamed Loki and told him to find a way out of the situation. Loki turned himself into a mare and lured the stallion away so that the giant could not complete the work on time.

Loki later gave birth to a grey foal with eight legs, which was named Sleipnir. He grew up to be a fine horse and became Odin's charger.

Loki brought nothing but trouble to Asgard and was always getting into mischief. On another occasion he cut off the beautiful golden hair of Thor's wife, Sif, while she was asleep. Thor was so angry that he made Loki go down into the depths of the Earth to the realm of Nifleheim to fetch some gold hair made by the dwarfs to replace it.

The Apples of Youth

The apples that the goddess Iduna carried in her magic casket were the secret of the Aesirs' eternal youth. Whenever the gods felt old age approaching, they had only to taste the apples to become young again.

The frost giants of Jotunheim knew about the apples and longed to be immortal too, but Iduna never left Asgard and so the apples remained safe there.

One day Loki was captured by an eagle, who was really the giant Thiassi in disguise. The giant refused to let Loki go until he promised to bring Iduna and her apples down to earth.

Loki was interested only in saving his own skin, so he quickly thought of a way of luring Iduna out of Asgard. He told her that he had seen golden apples on earth that were even more beautiful and powerful than her apples of youth. Iduna was so curious that she agreed to go with him to look. As soon as Iduna entered Midgard, the eagle swooped down out of the sky and carried her and the apples away.

It was not long before the effect of the apples wore off and the gods began to grow old and weak. They suspected Loki of betraying Iduna, and threatened him with instant death unless he rescued the goddess and the apples of youth immediately.

So Loki took the shape of a falcon and flew off to Thiassi's mountain home. He changed Iduna and her casket into a nut and clasping it between his claws, flew slowly back up towards Asgard. He was also getting older and could not fly fast.

The Aesir watched anxiously as Thiassi chased after him. As Loki landed inside the walls, they lit a great fire on the battlements of Asgard that scorched the eagle's wings and made him fall back to earth to his death. And so the gods were able to eat the apples of youth once more, and they have remained safely in Asgard ever since.

Thor visits the Giants

Many stories have been told of the mighty Thor's fights with the giants of Utgard in Jotunheim. Armed with his huge hammer Miolnir, iron gauntlets, and a magic girdle that gave him superhuman strength, he fought anyone who threatened to attack the Aesir, the gods of Asgard.

One day Thor received an invitation for himself and Loki to visit Utgard to talk about peace. Harnessing his two goats to his chariot, he drove off in a great thundercloud. Soon they entered Midgard, the home of men. As dusk started to fall Thor pulled up outside a farmhouse and asked for food and shelter for the night. The farmer welcomed them, but said he had very little food, in fact hardly enough for himself and his son, Thialfi.

'That doesn't matter,' said Thor, 'we'll eat my goats for supper.' He slaughtered both the animals and soon they were simmering in the cooking pot.

When it was time to eat, Thor spread out the skins of the goats and said 'As you eat, throw the bones on to the skin, and be careful not to break them.' But Thialfi, the farmer's son, was so hungry that he split one of the thigh bones in half and scraped out the marrow inside it.

In the morning Thor picked up all the bones in the goatskins and waved Miolnir over them. The two goats sprang to life again, but one of them limped.

'One of you has broken the thigh bone,' Thor roared, his eyes flashing fire. The terrified farmer went down on his knees and begged forgiveness.

'Have mercy on us,' he pleaded. 'Take my land, my farm, everything I own. But please spare our lives.'

Thor, seeing the man's fear, took pity on him and said, 'I will take Thialfi with me to be my servant, and you can look after my goats for me until I return.'

So Thor, Loki and Thialfi continued their journey on foot until they came to the sea, where a boat was waiting to take them to the shores of Jotunheim. There the three travellers set off through a dark forest until they came to a great hall that was completely open on one side. It was bitterly cold inside, but provided some shelter for the night. However none of them got much sleep because they were kept awake by a loud roaring noise.

When morning came Thor made his way out of the hall and saw a giant lying fast asleep. Now he realised that it was snoring they had heard in the night. Just then the giant woke and lumbered to his feet.

'Who are you?' Thor demanded. 'Your snoring has disturbed our sleep.'

'I am Skrymir,'
boomed the giant. 'I
have come to lead you
to Utgard. Have you seen
my glove?'

Thor looked around him,
but could not see it.

'Ah, there it is?' The giant
picked up what the travellers had
thought was a great hall and shook
Loki and Thialfi out of it. Then he
opened his bag and took out food for
breakfast, which he ate while the others
watched hungrily.

'Now follow me!' he commanded, and
strode away over the mountains. Thor and
his companions did their best to try and keep
up, and eventually caught up with him at
the edge of the forest. He lay stretched
out under a large oak.

'I'm too tired to bother about supper,' said
the giant, 'but here is my food bag. Help yourselves.'

He flung down the sack and rolled over on to his back.
Immediately his snoring rent the air like an earthquake.

Thor picked up the sack, but found he could not undo
it. The straps were so strong he could not loosen them;
neither could he cut through them with a knife.

'This giant is playing games with us,' he said angrily,
and brought his hammer down on Skrymir's head.

Skrymir stirred and yawned loudly. 'What was that?'
he said sleepily. 'Did a leaf fall on my head?' He was soon
snoring again, and the trees shook as if in a storm.

'I'll silence him,' said Thor, and gripping the hammer
firmly with both hands he swung it down right in the
middle of the giant's forehead.

Skrymir sat up slowly and rubbed his head. 'It must have been an acorn,' he said crossly, but soon went back to sleep.

Thor waited until his snores reached an ear-splitting crescendo and then rushed at the giant, whirling Miolnir round and round his head before landing a crashing great blow.

The giant was instantly awake. 'Drat those birds up in the oak tree,' he said. 'I thought I felt some droppings falling on me. Anyway, it's time we stirred ourselves. This is where I leave you. Turn to the east and you will reach Utgard before nightfall.'

Skrymir picked up his sack and strode off northwards towards the mountains. The four companions went on eastwards and came to an open plain. There stood a castle so high they had to throw back their heads to see the top of the walls. The great iron gates were locked, but Thor shook the bars and pulled with all his strength until he had made a gap that was big enough for them to squeeze through. Inside the castle walls there was a huge hall, and through the open door Thor could see a large number of giants sitting on benches round the walls. One giant sat alone on a throne at the end of the hall.

'I suppose this weakling here must be Thor from Asgard,' the giant said.

'I wonder if you are stronger than you look? And your companions – what can they do? We are all skilled in feats of strength and endurance. Which one of you will take up a challenge?'

Loki bravely stepped forward.'I will,' he cried. 'I will challenge anyone here to an eating contest.'

Utgardhaloki, the giant king, pointed to a giant sitting at the far end of the hall. 'Logi is our champion eater. He will compete with you.'

A huge wooden trough filled with meat was put in the centre of the hall. Loki sat down at one end, and Logi at the other. Each ate as fast he could, and they met exactly in the middle. Both had eaten every scrap of meat, but Logi had eaten the bones and the trough as well.

'I would say,' pronounced the giant king, 'that Logi is the winner.' He looked at Thialfi standing by Thor. 'What can this young man do?' he asked.

'I'll run a race with anyone who wants to try,' said Thialfi.

One of the younger giants stepped forward, and Utgardhaloki led the way out of the hall to a long strip of grass that made a good running track. At a sign from the king, Thialfi sprinted down the track as fast as his legs would carry him. But Hugi reached the winning post so far ahead of Thialfi that he was able to turn round and run back to meet him.

'So, Hugi runs swifter than Thialfi, and Logi is a faster eater than Loki,' said Utgardhaloki as he led the way back into the hall. 'But these were only small contests. I am sure that Thor will want to prove his strength. We have heard many tales of his great victories.'

'We came here to talk about peace, not war,' said Thor.

'But I am quite happy to challenge anyone to a drinking match.'

The giant king called for one of his servants to bring in the drinking horn. 'We think highly of any man who can drain this horn in one draught. Most of us here can empty it in two; and even the weakest youth can manage to finish in three.'

Thor gazed down into the long, narrow horn. He could not see the bottom, but he was very thirsty and did not doubt that he could drain it in one. He raised the horn to his lips and swallowed in great gulps. But when he lowered it, he saw that it was still almost as full as when he started.

'If I had been told that the great thunder god could only drink that much, I would never have believed it,' said Utgardhaloki.

'There must be magic in it,' said Thor angrily. 'Give me another test.'

Utgardhaloki shook his head and sighed. 'Well, I hardly dare to suggest such a small trial of strength for one so great as you, but the young giants here start by lifting my cat off the ground.'

As he said this an enormous grey cat sprang up from under the throne and stood spitting ferociously. Thor put one massive arm under the cat and began to lift. But the cat arched its back, and though he strained with all his strength, only one paw was raised from the ground.

All the giants laughed, and Utgardhaloki said 'Well, who would have believed that this mighty god is such a weakling?'

'You have been tricking me,' Thor roared angrily. 'I am willing to wrestle with anyone here.'

Utgardhaloki looked along the benches. 'There is no giant here who is weak enough to wrestle with you,' he scoffed. 'I had better call my old nurse, Elli, and let you wrestle with her.'

The giants chuckled as Elli hobbled into the hall. Thor could not bring himself to wrestle with an old woman, but Utgardhaloki insisted.

The moment Thor laid hands on her, he knew she was far stronger than she seemed. In an instant, Elli had grasped him round the waist with a grip of iron. Thor tottered and was brought to his knees.

'That's enough!' cried Utgardhaloki. 'I think Thor has shown that he cannot compete with us. Sit down now and join us at our feast.'

So the four travellers were found places on the crowded benches, and were given as much as they could eat. Then, exhausted, they fell asleep.

Next morning the giant king accompanied the travellers to the castle walls. 'Tell me, Thor,' said Utgardhaloki, 'what do you think of Utgard and the giants who live here? Do you admit that we are mightier than you?'

'I must confess that you have put me to shame,' said Thor sadly. 'And it was with a very different purpose that I came to visit Utgard for the Aesir.'

'Now I will tell you the truth,' said Utgardhaloki. 'I was Skrymir who met you in the forest. When you hit me with your hammer, I saved myself by placing a mountain in front of me. As for my food bag, it was fastened with iron wires made by trolls; you could not possibly have untied it.

'I also cheated over the contests. Loki was competing with fire, and when Thialfi ran against Hugi, he ran against my own thoughts. When you drank from the horn, the end of it was in the sea, which a thousand giants or gods could never drain. The cat you tried to lift was Jormungand, the serpent that circles the whole of Midgard. When you managed to raise a paw, we were all terrified. And Elli, my old nurse, is Death – no one can defeat her.'

As they reached the iron gates, Utgardhaloki said, 'It will be better for both of us if you do not visit again. If you come, I will use more magic. But if you stay away, then there may be peace between the Aesir and the giants.'

So the three companions made their way back to Midgard. Thor retrieved his chariot and goats, and with Loki beside him returned to Asgard determined to be more wary of the tricks of the giants in the future.

Balder and the Mistletoe

Balder the Beautiful, god of spring and sunlight, was one of the sons of Odin and Frigga. He was so sweet-tempered that he was loved by all the gods except Loki, who was jealous of him.

One night Balder dreamed that he was about to die. Frigga was so upset by this that she went round the world asking fire and water, trees and stones and all living things not to harm him. Then, since it appeared that nothing could hurt Balder any more, the gods amused themselves by throwing stones, darts and other weapons at him.

Loki the trickster discovered that Frigga had overlooked the mistletoe plant, since she had thought it too young to do harm. He made a twig of mistletoe into a dart and gave it to Hoder, the blind god. Not knowing that the dart was dangerous, Hoder threw it at Balder and he fell down dead.

All the other gods were speechless with horror, and Balder's wife Nanna died of grief. Balder's body was laid on a funeral pyre on his own ship, alongside the body of his wife and his horse. Frigga mourned the loss of her much-loved son and begged that someone should ride to Hel, the realm of the dead, and try to bring him back.

Hermod the Bold volunteered to do this, and he rode away on Odin's horse Sleipnir, journeying for nine days and nights through deep, dark valleys until he came to a golden bridge over the Echoing River. The maiden on guard there cried out to him that he could not be one of the dead, because the bridge resounded under his horse's hoofs.

Hermod told her that he was looking for Balder, and she directed him to Hel's gate, which Sleipnir cleared with an easy leap.

Hermod found Balder sitting in a great hall and begged that his spirit be allowed to come back. Hel, the goddess of the dead, agreed to release him on condition that all living things should mourn for him.

Hermod returned to Asgard with the ring Draupnir, which had been burnt on Balder's funeral pyre, as proof that he had fulfilled his mission. Messengers were sent all over the world asking everyone to show their love for Balder by weeping and mourning. The only one to refuse was Loki, who thus prevented Balder's return.

When Loki's refusal became known to the other gods they were beside themselves with anger. Loki fled to the mountains and hid in a river disguised as a fish. However he was caught in a magic net and Odin bound him to a rock with iron bands. A snake with poison dripping from its fangs was suspended above Loki's head. His faithful wife Siguna sat by his side holding a bowl to catch the drops, but each time she went to empty it the poison fell on Loki and made him twist his body so violently that the whole earth shook and produced earthquakes.

◁ Loki remained bound to the rock until he was able to break loose at the time of the battle of Ragnarok, the doom of the gods, when he led the giants and other monsters against Asgard.

Gods and Goddesses of China

The religious teachers of China, especially the Taoists and Buddhists, told stories to spread the beliefs of their faith. As a result the Chinese have a huge variety of deities, immortals and mythical rulers.

Oriental mythology is based on the idea of yin and yang, the two opposing parts which together make a harmonious whole. Yin and yang are found in all kinds of opposites – such as east and west, moon and sun, fire and water, dark and light, male and female.

YU-TI

According to one Taoist tradition, Yu-ti August Person of Jade was the ruler of heaven and the creator of mankind. His principal assistant was Tung-Yueh, Great Emperor of the Eastern Peak and the source of yang. Tung-Yueh was in charge of a host of minor deities who controlled every minute detail of ordinary life.

THE KITCHEN GOD

The chief deity of the family and home was Tsao Chun, the Kitchen God. On New Year's Eve he reported to heaven on each member of the household, so it was important to keep him in a good mood with offerings of honey and sweet cakes.

△ Yu-Ti was also called Yu-Huang-Shang-Ti or the August [very noble] Supreme Emperor of Jade, and as Lao-Tien-Yeh (Father Heaven).

KUAN TI

The role of Kuan Ti, god of war, was to prevent war rather than to encourage it. His other duty was to dispense justice. The executioner's sword was always kept in his temple.

Kuan Ti was also a patron of literature, and he was often called upon to make predictions about the future. He was invoked during the seasons of spring and summer.

THE PEACHES OF IMMORTALITY

◁ T'ao Hua Hsiennui was the spirit of the peach blossom and the deity worshipped in the second month of spring. She was often invoked before a marriage to ensure that the new member of the family would not bring disharmony into the household.

King Tung Wang-Kung of the East represented the male yang element. He was said to keep a record of all immortal beings. His wife Hsi Wang Mu, Queen of the West represented the female yin. She lived in a wonderful nine-storey jade palace surrounded by a beautiful garden. The queen created new immortals by giving virtuous humans a Peach of Immortality from her garden. However there were so few suitable mortals that the peaches only ripened every six thousand years.

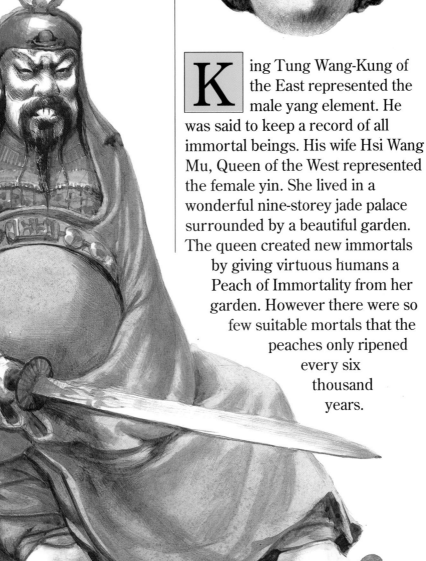

◁◁ Kuan Ti was originally a real person – a general in the Imperial Chinese Army, who died in AD 220. He was proclaimed a god after his death. The sword which he carries here was called Black Dragon and was supposed to have had magical powers.

THE EIGHT IMMORTALS

Part of the Taoist tradition was the worship of the Eight Immortals or Ba Xian. The best known of these immortals is Lu Tong-Pin, who dreamed that he was killed by a brigand and therefore decided to renounce the world to study Taoism. He is shown with a sword, and is dressed as a scholar.

Lu Tong-Pin taught the Taoist doctrine to another of the immortals, Han Xiang-Zhu. Li Thieh-Kuai, a cripple with an iron crutch, was also a disciple of Lao Tzu, the founder of Taoism.

Among the other immortals were Zhong-Li Kuan, who is shown with a fan, and a wealthy young man called Kao Kuo-Jiu who was his disciple and is shown carrying a rattle.

He Xian-Ku was a young girl who is shown with a ladle and a lotus. Lan Kai-He, a ragged street singer with one bare foot, was taken up to heaven by a stork.

Lastly Zhang Kuo-Lan was an old man who had a donkey that could walk thousands of miles in a day. When he was not travelling it could be folded up like a piece of paper.

The Story of Monkey

Hsuan Tsang was a Chinese scholar of the seventh century. The story of his journey to India to study Buddhism is told in a novel called *The Story of Monkey*.

A long time ago, on a mountain-top far away in the east, an egg was fertilized by the wind. When the egg hatched, a monkey was born. He organized all the other monkeys into a kingdom and became their ruler.

Monkey had magical powers. He could fly and change his shape. With his magic sword he travelled far and wide until he had conquered the whole world. A great feast was given in Monkey's honour, but he drank too much and was captured by demons and taken to hell. When he escaped, he crossed out his own name and those of all the other monkeys from the judgement register.

The gods summoned Monkey and asked him to explain his behaviour. But he made himself immortal by eating one of the Peaches of Immortality and started trying to conquer heaven, too. In despair, the Jade Emperor sent for the Buddha and asked for his help.

'What makes you think you should be ruler of heaven?' the Buddha demanded of the unrepentant Monkey.

'Because I am the most powerful individual,' Monkey replied. 'I am immortal, I can fly, I can change into seventy-two different shapes, and I can leap 100,000 li [about 54,000 kilometres].'

'I doubt whether you could even leap across my palm,' said the Buddha.

In a single bound Monkey sprang right across heaven to a mountain at the end of the universe. Then he sprang back again.

'That mountain is no more than the base of my finger,' said the Buddha scornfully. 'You have not even escaped from the palm of my hand.'

The Buddha shut Monkey up in a magic mountain that he had created. But, when Hsuan Tsang left on his pilgrimage to India, Monkey was released to travel with Hsuan Tsang as his servant. An iron helmet was fitted on his head which tightened whenever he was tempted to misbehave.

Despite many temptations, Monkey guarded his master safely through many adventures and helped bring back the Buddhist scriptures to China.

The Dragon Gods

According to Chinese mythology, dragons control the elements of water and air, and were responsible for making rain. This story explains why mere mortals should never be put in charge of such an important task and what happened when one was.

Li Ching was hunting deer in the Huo Mountains when night began to fall. Losing his way in the dark, he plodded on wearily for hours before seeing a light in the distance.

As he got closer he saw a stately mansion with a red gate and a high wall. He knocked on the gate and a servant came out to ask what he wanted.

'Ask your master if I might have a bed for the night,' begged Li Ching.

'Both gentlemen are away,' said the servant, 'but I will ask the mistress.'

The man went in and returned soon afterwards. 'The mistress would not agree at first,' he said, 'but as it is a very dark night and you have lost your way, she has decided to offer you hospitality.'

The mistress was a refined lady of middle years, who welcomed Li Ching and said, 'I expect my sons to return at any moment. The elder has gone to a wedding and the younger is escorting his sister on a journey.'

Presently a meal was served, and two maids brought a mat and bedding so that Li Ching could retire for the night. About midnight he heard a loud knocking at the gate and then a ringing voice called, 'It is Heaven's will that the eldest son shall make rain around these mountains for seven hundred li. The appropriate amount should be distributed by the fifth watch.'

After a short time had elapsed a servant appeared and summoned Li Ching into the mistress's presence. 'Honoured guest,' said the lady, 'I must tell you that this is not an ordinary house, but a dragons' palace. An order has come from Heaven to make rain, but my sons have not returned. Would you be willing to carry out the task?'

'I am only a poor mortal, not a god,' replied Li Ching. 'But if you will teach me how, I am willing to obey.'

The mistress told the servant to bring a piebald horse with a rain bottle tied to its saddle. 'Let the horse find its own way, and when it rears and neighs, take just one drop of water from the bottle and place it on the mane. Be sure not to take more than a drop.'

Li Ching mounted the horse, which flew off into the air above the clouds. A terrific wind blew, and thunder roared beneath his feet. Whenever the horse reared, he put a drop of water on its mane.

After a time Li Ching saw down below the mountain village where he lived, and he thought of the drought that had been plaguing the farmers for some months. I must not be so frugal in dispensing the rain, he thought, and sprinkled twenty drops on the horse's mane.

When Li Ching finally returned to the Dragons' Palace he was greeted by his hostess, who was in great distress.

'How could you make such a mistake?' she wept. 'I told you to dispense just one drop when the horse reared and neighed. One drop in Heaven is the equivalent of several centimetres of rain on earth, so that that village has been completely flooded in the middle of the night.'

And when Li Ching eventually returned to his home, he found his village sunk under the deep waters of a lake, and no sign of any survivors.

Gods and Goddesses of Japan

Japanese mythology is contained in two old books called the *Kigi*. They were compiled on the instructions of Emperor Tenmu, who wanted official records of the imperial family's descent from Amaterasu, the sun goddess.

The Japanese word for a god, Kami, was used for anything that possessed supernatural powers or great beauty. Mountains, caves, rocks, waterfalls, rivers, trees, animals and humans could all be worshipped as Kami.

IN AND YO

Like the Chinese, the Japanese people believe that everything has two separate and opposing elements which together make a whole.

The female element, associated with the night, is called In. Yo, the male element, is the day and light.

In is the earth and water; Yo is the sun and wind.

Each element is powerless and meaningless without the other. Numerically, In exists in all even numbers; Yo in the odd numbers. All numbers are separate and yet are useless for calculation without all other numbers, so that In and Yo must always work together to achieve an end.

IZANAGI AND IZANAMI

According to Japanese mythology, at the beginning of time there was Chaos, and the universe resembled an egg. Gradually the light transparent part of the egg, the Yo, rose to the top, while the heavy, thick, yellow In sank down and became the earth. The newly

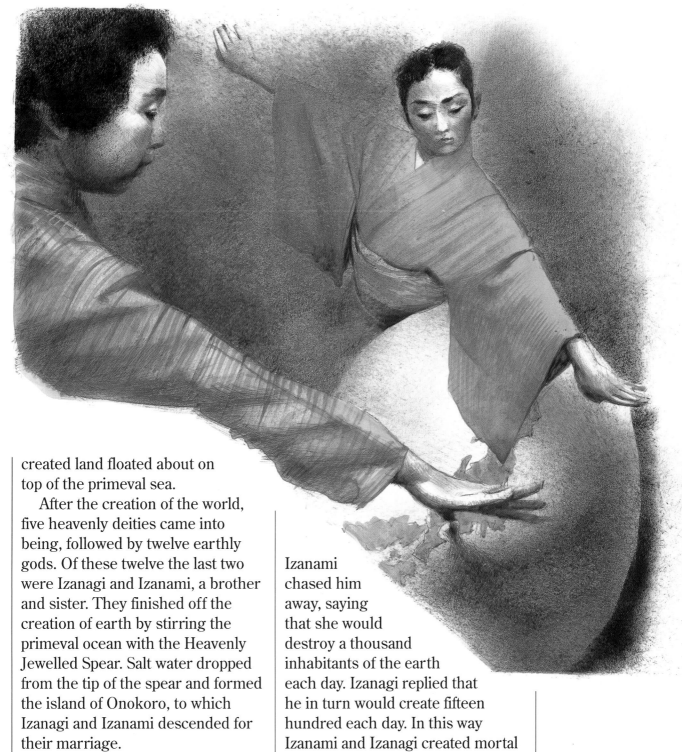

created land floated about on top of the primeval sea.

After the creation of the world, five heavenly deities came into being, followed by twelve earthly gods. Of these twelve the last two were Izanagi and Izanami, a brother and sister. They finished off the creation of earth by stirring the primeval ocean with the Heavenly Jewelled Spear. Salt water dropped from the tip of the spear and formed the island of Onokoro, to which Izanagi and Izanami descended for their marriage.

This pair produced the fourteen islands of Japan, and forty deities related to the winds, the sea, rivers, mountains, crops, fertility and houses. Finally Izanami died of a burning fever after giving birth to the god of fire. She went down to the Underworld – Yomi, the Land of Gloom – but Izanagi followed her there in spite of her protests.

Izanami chased him away, saying that she would destroy a thousand inhabitants of the earth each day. Izanagi replied that he in turn would create fifteen hundred each day. In this way Izanami and Izanagi created mortal life and death.

Izanagi went on to give birth to Amaterasu-omikama the sun goddess, Tsuki-yumi the moon god and Susano-Wo the storm god. Amaterasu and Tsuki-yumi obeyed Izanagi's command to govern heaven and the night, but Susano-Wo refused to govern the sea and was expelled to the underworld.

Why the Sun hid in a Cave

Amaterasu-omikama the sun goddess was the most important deity in Japan. Before going down to the underworld for ever, Susano-Wo the storm god visited his sister in heaven and caused great upheaval and destruction in the skies. Amaterasu was so angry by his actions that she shut herself up in a cave and refused to come out.

Heaven and earth, thus deprived of sunlight, were plunged into perpetual darkness. This caused all sorts of problems, so the other gods and goddesses met to discuss the best way of appeasing the sun goddess.

It was Omoigane, the god of wisdom, who thought of a way out. A fine mirror, a three-metre rope of jewels, and offerings were hung from the branches of a tree that grew outside the cave. Then some of the goddesses started to sing and dance, and the others laughed and applauded loudly.

Amaterasu opened a narrow crack in the cave and asked why they were celebrating. The gods held up the mirror so that she could see her reflection in it and told her that they had found a new goddess who was superior in beauty and in power to Amaterasu.

Overcome with jealousy, Amaterasu came closer to the mouth of the cave. As she did so Tajikara-wo, the god of strength, caught her by the hand and pulled her out. And so heaven and earth became light again.

▷ Some people say that Amaterasu's emergence from the cave represents the return of spring after the darkness of winter. Others think of it as a description of a solar eclipse.

Susano-Wo, the Storm God

After Susano-Wo was banished from heaven for ever, he descended to Izumo Province in Japan, where he met an old couple who were in great distress. Their eighth daughter Kushi-inada was about to be sacrificed to an enormous serpent which had already devoured her seven elder sisters. This fearsome monster had eight heads and eight tails, and was so huge that it spanned eight valleys and mountain peaks.

The god promised to save Kushi-inada from the serpent provided that he could have her as his wife. The old couple agreed readily to this bargain. So Susano-Wo transformed the girl into a comb, which he stuck in the knot of his hair. Then he filled eight barrels with rice wine.

When the serpent appeared each of its eight heads drank up one barrel of wine. As soon as it was completely drunk, Susano-Wo drew his sword and chopped the monster into tiny pieces.

In one of its eight tails he found a magical sword, called Kusanagi-no-Tsurugi or Grasscutter, which he gave to his sister Amaterasu as a peace offering.

Then Susano-Wo married Kushi-inada and they lived in a palace at Suga in Izumo. They produced over eighty sons, including O-Kuni-Nushi who ruled the earth until Amaterasu sent her grandson, Ninigi, to be the first emperor of Japan. Susano-Wo's children were also the ancestors of the ruling family of Izumo Province.

▽ Susano-Wo, the god of storms, was always causing trouble. Before he was banished from heaven, his troublesome disposition brought him into conflict with almost everyone who crossed his path.

NINIGI

The family of the Japanese emperor was supposed to be descended from Amaterasu through her grandson Ninigi. The legend says that the sun goddess sent Ninigi to earth with some rice from the sacred rice field, so that he could grow rice on earth.

She also gave him the mirror and jewels that had been used to lure her out of the cave, and the sword from the serpent's tail. These three objects became the emblems of imperial power in Japan.

Prince Ninigi descended to earth on Mount Takachiho in Kyushu Province. The god of the mountain offered him his two daughters, one of whom was ugly and one beautiful.

Ninigi chose to marry only the younger beautiful one, but he should have taken the elder one too, to ensure long life. As a result of his choice future emperors of Japan had relatively short lives.

▷▷ Nai-No-Kami was recognized as a god following a series of bad earthquakes in Japan in AD 599. Rituals for his worship were sent to all the provinces with instructions that proper respect was to be shown to this god who had such powers of destruction.

JIZO BOSATSU

One of the most popular gods of Japan is Jizo Bosatsu, who was originally the Indian Bodhisattva Kshitigarbha, who had special charge of the Buddhist purgatories.

He protects humanity from peril and, in particular, he looks after children, and women while they are giving birth. He also rescues souls from hell and transports them up to heaven.

Jizo is usually portrayed as a Buddhist monk, but sometimes he is shown as a Chinese soldier carrying a crozier and a pearl. He was one of the many deities that were adopted in Japan when Buddhism spread there from China in the sixth century.

There are also six jizos or bodhisattvas who guard the roads that people must travel after their death and judgement. These roads lead to Jigoku (or Hell), and the worlds of the demons, of animals, of the anti-gods (or asuras), of humans and of the devas (or gods).

NAI-NO-KANI

From time to time Japan is afflicted with terrible earthquakes. These are said to occur when Nai-No-Kani, the god of earthquakes, is displeased with the behaviour of humankind and decides to punish them.

The Invisible Samurai

Many years ago, in Kyoto, there was a young samurai who worshipped regularly at the temple of the goddess Kwannon, who is also called Kuan Yin. One evening the samurai was coming back from the temple at nightfall when he saw a number of men carrying lighted torches crossing the bridge towards him. They must be escorting an important nobleman, he thought, and hurried to get out of the way.

As the procession got nearer he saw that the torch-carriers were not men at all, but kappi and oni – the evil spirits of Japan. Some had one eye, some had horns or horses' heads, some had extra hands, and some had only one foot and hopped. The oni spat on the samurai as they went past, but he was just relieved that he had not been killed.

The samurai hurried home to tell his family about the encounter, but when he went indoors, his wife and children looked right through him as if he was not there. Neither did they answer when he spoke to them. It was some time before the samurai realized that when the oni spat on him, he had become invisible.

Several days passed, and the samurai decided the

▽ Onis are the terrible messengers of Emma Hoo, the king of Jigoku (the Japanese Hell). They often have red and green bodies and horses' heads. Kappi are ugly little dwarves, who hide under bridges to catch unsuspecting travellers.

Kwannon, or Kuan Yin, was originally a male Indian deity, who was adopted by the Japanese Buddhists about AD 600. By about 1100, he had become a female deity who was invoked in situations of danger and by people who wanted children.

only thing he could do was to go into a retreat. He went to the temple in Kyoto and prayed, 'Kwannon, save me. I have worshipped you for many years and put my trust in you. Now please help me to regain my natural form.'

The samurai ate rice and slept by the side of other people in the retreat, but none of them were aware of him.

One night, shortly before dawn, a monk appeared to the samurai in his dreams. He said, 'Leave this retreat first thing in the morning and do as the first person you meet tells you.'

At dawn the samurai left the temple and the first person that he met was a herd boy leading an ox. The boy looked at him and said, 'Come with me.'

The samurai was overjoyed that someone could see him, and followed the boy happily through the city.

Soon they came to a large mansion. They went inside and right into the women's quarters where the samurai saw a beautiful young woman lying in bed. She was obviously ill and in great pain. Her parents and maids were weeping and praying over her. Just then a priest arrived. As soon as the ox boy saw the priest, he ran out of the house at top speed.

The priest sat close to the sick girl and began to chant. A chill went right through the samurai's body and his hair stood on end. Then his clothing caught fire, and as it burned the samurai screamed.

At that moment he became fully visible again, and everyone was surprised and horrified to see a strange man standing there.

'Who are you? How did you get in?' they demanded, as they dragged him away from the sickbed and bound his hands.

Then the priest said, 'Do not harm this man, for he has received the favour of the goddess Kwannon. Release him at once.'

So they released the samurai, and as he was explaining to them what had happened to him, everyone suddenly realized that the sick girl had also recovered. It was as though her illness had been simply wiped away.

Neither the young lady nor the samurai were ill ever again – such are the benefits with which Kwannon favours her faithful worshippers.

Latin America

The ancient civilizations worshipped many gods, but believed in a single creation. In many parts of Latin America there was a belief in more than one creation, or age, of which the present world is but one.

In Latin American creation myths a central theme is finding the right material from which to make human beings. One traditional story says that maize was chosen for this all-important role; another says that the substance used was bonemeal.

AZTEC GODS

When the Aztecs first came to live in Mexico in the thirteenth century, they were hunters. They worshipped sky gods, in particular Huitzilpochtli, or Blue Hummingbird, the god of the noonday sun. Their temples, built from huge blocks of stone, were raised as high as possible so that they could be near to the sky gods.

The Aztecs' religious customs were very savage. They believed

△ The Aztecs' chief god was Blue Hummingbird or Huitzilpochtli. He was said to be one of the four sons of Texcatlipoca. He was a god of war and led the Aztecs across Mexico to found their great city of Tenochtitlan on the site of what is now Mexico City.

that the gods watched them constantly and would become angry if they did not carry out sacrifices and festivals at the right time. They thought that the gods demanded the sacrifice of human beings. Sometimes thousands were necessary, and the priests would sacrifice prisoners captured in the wars by tearing out their hearts, which the gods were supposed to need as food. Every year, too, they chose one of the most beautiful of their young men as a special victim.

As their empire grew, the Aztecs learned of new gods from other tribes and introduced them to their city to be honoured in festivals.

TLALOC

When farming became important to the Aztecs, and their crops needed rain, they began to worship Tlaloc,

the Toltec god of rain and thunder, as well. Tlaloc is always portrayed with a mask, long teeth and goggling frog-like eyes.

Tlaloc's rain was not freely given, however, it had to be bargained for. In exchange for the rain Tlaloc was offered the blood of sacrificed victims every day.

QUETZALCOATL

As the Aztecs became more settled in Mexico they learned writing and astrology from the Toltecs.

The Toltec god of learning was Quetzalcoatl, the feathered serpent god (opposite). He appeared in many forms, but always with his symbols, the quetzal bird and a serpent. Sometimes he was a handsome young man dressed in a cloak of feathers from the quetzal bird. At other times he arched himself across the heavens as the Plumed Serpent.

Quetzalcoatl had arrived in Tula, the capital of the Toltecs, as a mysterious stranger. He brought with him the arts and culture – painting, weaving, dancing, poetry and writing. He was also the creator of all life and god of the wind. In time he revealed to his people the gold that lay under the earth, and taught them how to fashion it into jewellery and beautiful ornaments.

The feathered serpent god rejected human sacrifice, so under his rule the Toltec people enjoyed both wealth and happiness. This made him unpopular with the other gods, in particular with Tezcatlipoca the warrior god.

TEZCATLIPOCA

This warrior god's name means 'mirror' (*tezcatli*) and 'smoke' (*poca*). He is club-footed, but this deformity is covered up by the mirror-smoke of his name.

Tezcatlipoca was jealous of the people's love for Quetzalcoatl, so he caused thousands of them to be killed in natural disasters. He then began to turn men against each other in bloody wars and taught them to be greedy for gold instead of enjoying it for its beauty.

Quetzalcoatl began to despair of the people's behaviour, and eventually he, too, fell from grace when Tezcatlipoca made him drunk. He decided to leave Tula for a while, promising to return again some time in the future.

When the Spanish conquistadors appeared across the eastern horizon the Aztecs thought that Quetzalcoatl had returned and welcomed them with great joy. But Tezcatlipoca had played a final trick on the unsuspecting people. The Spaniards were fierce and greedy invaders who destroyed the empire founded by Quetzalcoatl.

▷ Tezcatlipoca was the last son of the Great Mother of the Thirteenth Heaven in Central American mythology. The 400 star gods whom the Great Mother had borne before him, plotted to kill Tezcatlipoca at the moment of his birth. But Tezcatlipoca emerged from his mother's womb fully-armed and with the help of his sister, Coyolxauhqui, defeated his jealous brothers.

Tezcatlipoca acquired more guises and names than any other deity. Two of these were Yaotl, or warrior, and Yoalli Ehecatl, or night wind. In these two guises he was associated with death, warfare and darkness.

INCA GODS

The great gods of the Incas of Peru were the powers of nature, especially the sun god Inti, the giver of food and strength, and his wife Kilya, the moon goddess.

Another important god was Ilyap'a, the weather god, who was depicted as a man with a sling. He made rain fall by shattering a pitcher of water with his slingshot.

The capital of the Inca Empire was Cuzco, the sacred city of the sun. Every important Inca town had a great carved stone, called an intihuatana, which marked the days on which the sun passed overhead at noon. At this moment the upright in the centre of the stone cast no shadow and it was a time for great celebration.

The high priest, attended by Sun Virgins, poured out an offering of *chicha* (beer made from fermented maize) while the people chanted a hymn to the sun, thanking him for his warmth and light and for his son, the Sapa Inca. The ruler of the Inca empire was regarded as a god and was supposed by the people to be descended from the sun.

△ The first emperor of the Incas was Manco Capac, who married his sister, Mama Ocllo. They were the children of the sun god and emerged from a cave high in the Andes to lead the Inca people.

EL DORADO

When the Spaniards conquered Peru in the sixteenth century they found temples and palaces crammed with gold images, and people wearing gold jewellery and eating from golden plates.

Stories soon began to circulate about El Dorado, the golden man, who was said to be chief of a tribe fabulously rich in gold. Each morning the priests coated his body with gold dust so that he walked among his subjects like a glistening gold statue. Each evening he washed the gold dust off in a lake.

On certain days of each year, it was rumoured that the people performed a special ritual of throwing golden objects into the lake as sacrifices to their ruler. The bottom of the lake must therefore be thick with gold dust and precious trinkets.

Many Spanish explorers went to Central or South America during the sixteenth century to search for El Dorado, and many more hopeful adventurers have gone there since.

VIRACOCHA

In Inca mythology the place of creation was Lake Titicaca. The creator was the god Viracocha, who is portrayed as a bearded white-skinned man.

Viracocha made figures of clay and painted on them the clothes that each different nation on earth was to wear. To each nation he gave a language and the seeds they were to sow. As the world was still dark, he then made the sun, moon and stars and ordered them to go to Lake Titicaca and from there to ascend to their places in heaven.

As the sun, in the form of a man, was rising to heaven he called out to the Inca chief, Manco Capac, 'You and your descendants are to be kings and rulers, and are to conquer many nations.'

The story goes that Manco Capac was given a head-dress and a battle-axe and founded a new city where Cuzco now stands.

◁ Viracocha was represented in the shrine at Cuzco in Peru, where the Spanish conquerors first saw him, as a golden statue about the height of a ten year-old boy.

North America

Before European settlers arrived in North America, the native people lived in tribes. Each tribe had its own gods and mythology, and these were closely connected to the crops, animals and landscape of the area in which the tribe lived. Maize and bison were important to the tribes who lived in the Great Plains, and these are linked together in many of their myths. For the Pueblo people of the hot, dry Americas Southwest, water was vital for the growth of corn. The mythology of the Pueblo people is therefore principally concerned with rain and the fertility of their crops.

How Raven Created Earth

Myths about the origin of the Earth vary throughout North America. The Inuit people of the Northwest Coast say that at the very beginning a raven was born out of the darkness and chaos.

To begin with, Raven was small and weak. He searched around in the dark trying to get his bearings, and felt water, grass and trees. Having pondered for some time about what made the grass grow, and about who he was, Raven eventually realized that he must be Tulugaukuk, the Raven Father, the creator of all life.

Raven flew down through the darkness and found a new land, which he covered with growing things. He called the new land Earth. One day, while surveying his handiwork, he noticed a giant pea pod. The pod split open and out popped a man, the first Eskimo or Inuit. Raven created two animals, the musk-ox and the caribou, for the man to eat, but told him he must treat the animals with respect and not deliberately harm them. He then continued creating other animals, and then finally he created a woman to be the man's companion.

Raven taught the man how to build a house and a canoe, and the woman how to make clothes from the skins of the animals. Soon the first man and woman produced a child. Three more men popped out of pea pods, and soon there were many children. These new people began to kill more animals than were necessary and to fight among themselves. They paid no attention to anything that Raven said.

He therefore returned to the sky that he had come from, causing darkness to cover the Earth once more. However, from time to time he allowed the sun to peep through the darkness, providing enough light for the people to hunt.

Back in his own land in the sky, Raven took a snow goose for his wife. They had a son called Raven Boy. One day, while Raven slept, Raven Boy opened the chest where the sun was stored and soared away into the darkness, carrying the sun with him. Raven flew after his son, begging him to come back and not hide the sun for ever.

Raven Boy set the sun back in its place so that light could return to Earth once more, but with a flip of his wing he sent the sky spinning round the Earth, carrying the sun with it and so creating day and night.

LADY HANGING HAIR

Another legend of the Northwest tells of a gentle goddess called Lady Hanging Hair. She lived among the trees near a dangerous whirlpool, Keagyihl Depguesk, and tried to protect people from being sucked down into its waters.

One day Lady Hanging Hair arranged a great feast and invited all the powerful gods of nature to attend. The wind god roared along in a great gust of wind, the storm god came with thunder and lightning, the fire god came in a blaze of flames, and the goddesses showed off their particular skills.

All the gods and goddesses took their places at table. When they had eaten and were in a good humour, Lady Hanging Hair suggested that the power of Keagyihl Depguesk should be reduced. Each god and goddess gave their opinion in turn, and finally they agreed to give the earth a good shake which would rearrange the rocks in the river and reduce the force of water flowing through the whirlpool.

So the wind god blew a gale, the storm god cast a thunderbolt, the rain god flooded the land, and the fire god caused a forest fire. When the elements subsided, the river was calm and the terrible whirlpool was no more than a gentle ripple.

THUNDERBIRD

The tribes of the eastern forests thought that the earth was flat and rested on the back of a giant turtle. The sky was the roof of the world, and it was also the lowest tier of heaven, where the thunder god lived.

This was a giant bird with a human face, sometimes portrayed with an extra head protruding from its abdomen. Thunderbird had killed people and destroyed the crops, but it also brought the rain to make crops grow.

One story tells of two hunters who travelled up a river until they arrived at a lake high in the mountains. As night fell they set up camp and lay down to sleep. In the middle of the night the hunters were woken by a loud noise and saw an enormous bird rise from the lake. As it spread its wings there was a roar of thunder, and lightning flashed from its beak.

Down in the village the rest of the tribe witnessed the storm and feared for the hunters who were so close to the mighty Thunderbird. There was much rejoicing when the men returned unharmed.

The Corn Maidens

The Zuni are a Pueblo tribe, who live in western New Mexico. The corn maiden ceremony, one of their most sacred rites, was held every four years at harvest time.

When the ancestors of the Zuni people came up from the underworld they were accompanied by ten lovely corn maidens who were invisible to the human eye. The maidens travelled with the tribe for four years.

Then, at Shipololo, the place of mist and cloud, they were discovered by two witches who had been the last people to emerge from the world below. The witches gave the maidens seeds of maize and squash, and transformed them into human shape. The Zuni ancestors continued on their journey, leaving the corn maidens behind at Shipololo in a magical dance-bower made of cedar wood and roofed with clouds.

One day the maidens were discovered by Kowwituma and Watsusii, twin sons of the sun god. The sun priest told the twins to bring the corn maidens before the people to dance. The maidens danced in a courtyard decorated with cornmeal paintings of clouds, waving bright stalks of corn with their white plume-like leaves. As they danced, all the people fell asleep.

Payatami, the little god of flowers and butterflies, had also come to watch. He was charmed by the lovely maidens, especially by the Yellow Corn Maiden. However the corn maidens were able to read his thoughts, and kept dancing until he, too, had fallen asleep. As day dawned, the maidens fled away to the Mist and Cloud Spring, where they hid under the wings of the ducks.

With the corn maidens gone, the harvest failed and there was a great famine. The Zuni begged Kowwituma and Watsusii to bring the maidens back. The twins enlisted the help of their father's musician, Bitsitsi. He descended to earth on a star and told the maidens how much they were missed, and that in future they would be treated with great honour and respect.

The maidens were eventually persuaded to return. Led by Bitsitsi, they came again to the people, each holding a stalk of corn, and danced from dawn to dusk to the music of the repentant Payatami's flute.

Soon the crops grew again and the famine ended. Since then, the beauty and dancing of the corn maidens have been celebrated in Zuni ritual every four years.

COYOTE

O ne of the Navajo people's chief gods is Coyote. He is a mischievous and cunning deity who plays all sorts of tricks on human beings in order to teach them the ways of the world.

In many stories Coyote is shown as being deceitful and greedy. He is often outwitted by those he tries to trick, and he is never grateful to those who help him. Yet he is also a great magician, and manages to bring order to the world.

Coyote and the Five Worlds

The Navajo believed that humans and the spirit world should live in a harmonious relationship with each other. If this harmony was upset, then disaster came as flood, famine or disease.

A ccording to the Navajo story of the creation, the present world that we live in is the fifth world. The first world was completely dark, and in it there were only three beings – the first man, the first woman and Coyote. The first world was too small for them, so they travelled to the second world.

In the second world the east was dark, but in the south it was blue, in the west yellow, and in the north white. A god lived in each of the four colours. Sometimes the darkness in the east overshadowed the whole world, bringing night. But soon the other colours would appear again, bringing day.

When the three travellers arrived in the second world, the sun caused trouble by trying to make love to the first woman. Coyote called on the gods who lived in the north, south, east and west to pass judgement. They decided that the second world was too small, and that the travellers should climb up to the third world, where there would be enough room for the sun to be completely separated from the first woman for ever.

The third world was a spacious and beautiful place, rather like the earth we know today. At the corners of the world there were four mountains, with people and animals living on the slopes. The people welcomed the newcomers and said that there would be peace and harmony in the third world as long as Tieholtsodi the water monster was not upset.

Coyote ignored the warning, and set off to look for the monster. Beside a lake he found two of Tieholtsodi's children, and took them away. When the monster found they were gone, he guessed that they must have been stolen by the newcomers, so he took his revenge by creating a flood. The people tried to escape from the flood waters by piling the four mountains on top of each other in the middle of the land. When the waters rose still higher, they planted a giant reed on top of the piled-up mountains. All the people and animals climbed up the reed into the fourth world. The last one up was the turkey, whose tail feathers were washed pale by the flood.

The fourth world was larger than the third. It had mountains and seas, and across the central plain flowed a wide river. Human beings lived on the north bank of the river, and animals on the south bank. Trouble soon came when the women and the men began to quarrel about who worked hardest. The women claimed that they

not only looked after the children, but made all the clothes and cooking pots, cooked the meat and planted the fields. The men argued that they did all the hunting to provide the meat, built houses, cleared the land for planting, and – most important – performed all the rituals and dances to make the crops grow.

Since they could not agree, the men and women decided to separate. The men built a boat and sailed across the river to the south bank, leaving the women to grow their own crops without the benefit of rituals and dances.

The separation lasted for four years. During that time the women's crops grew poorer and poorer. The men produced better crops, and had plenty of meat from hunting, but were tired of having to do everything for themselves. Eventually the men and women realized that they needed each other, and joined up together again. From then on they lived more or less harmoniously, with much greater understanding.

However, Coyote still held captive the two children of the water monster, and the world was soon threatened by another flood. Again the mountains were piled on each other, and a great reed was planted up to the fifth world. The people and animals surged up the reed, each carrying a bundle of their most precious possessions. Suddenly Tieholtsodi appeared in their midst and demanded to see what was in the bundles. In this way Coyote was forced to reveal the stolen children.

When the three monsters had swum away, the people found themselves standing on an island in the middle of a swamp. They prayed to the god of blackness in the east, and he cut open the surrounding cliffs with his knife so that the water drained away. They prayed to the god of the winds, and he sent a fierce gale that dried out the earth and made it hard.

Then the people threw the sun and moon up into the sky, but the sun stood still so that everything was in danger of being burned. Coyote told the people that the sun must be placated by human death, otherwise he could not move. A chief's wife offered herself to the sun, and as her life ebbed away the sun moved once more.

This was the first time that human beings had encountered death, and they were a little afraid. But looking down, they saw the dead woman sitting happily by the river of the fourth world, combing her hair. So they accepted the fact that death would be the inevitable end to their existence in the fifth world, but then they could look forward to returning to the fourth world.

Gods and Goddesses of Africa

I n Africa, each tribal group has its own religion and pantheon of gods. Each also has its own version of the creation story. In some areas of Africa, the people believe that the first man appeared from below the earth. The Ashanti of West Africa say that he came up through a large wormhole, the Herero of Kenya that he emerged from a tree, and the Zulus of South Africa that he burst out of an exploding reed. Other tribes say that a god created mankind, with the help of one or more deputies, or kindred spirits.

MAWU AND LISA

A ccording to the Fon tribe of Dahomey and Benin in West Africa, a creative spirit called Nana-Buluku created the twin gods Mawu and Lisa.

Mawu, the female twin, is associated with the moon, night, sleep, motherhood and gentleness. She lived in the west. Lisa, the male twin, is associated with the sun, day, heat, strength, and the more vigorous side of life. He lived in the east. This pair came together in an eclipse and gave birth to all the other gods, most of whom were also twins.

Mawu and Lisa were at the head of the most important pantheon of gods, the sky. They gave each set of twins a domain to rule over.

The first set of twins was entrusted with the rule of the Earth. The twins of Storm were told to stay in the sky and rule over the thunder and lightning. The Iron twins cleared the forests and gave mankind tools to cultivate the land.

A fourth set of twins lived in the ocean and controlled the waves and sea life. The fifth set of twins were sent into the bush where they ruled over the birds and beasts.

Legba's Revenge

Legba was the youngest son of Mawu and Lisa. Like every youngest son in mythology, he was clever and cunning, and he was always playing tricks on his parents, brothers and sisters.

In the beginning Legba lived with his parents on earth and did as he was told. Sometimes he was told to do something harmful, and then the people blamed Legba for it and came to hate him. They never gave him credit for the good things, but thanked Mawu and Lisa instead.

Legba got tired of this and asked his father why he should always take the blame for the evil things he had done, since he was only carrying out the divine will. Lisa replied that it was right that the ruler of a kingdom should be thanked for good things and his servants blamed for evil.

Legba decided that he would get his revenge. One day he went to his father and told him that he had heard that thieves were planning to steal the yams out of his garden. The god called all of humankind together and warned them that whoever stole his yams would be killed.

Under cover of darkness Legba crept into Lisa's house and stole his sandals. Putting them on his own feet, he then went out into the garden and dug up all the yams. It had recently rained, and the footprints that he left were clearly visible.

In the morning Legba reported the theft, pointing out that it would be easy to find the thief from the footprints. All the people were called together, but nobody's feet were large enough to fit the prints. Then Legba suggested that perhaps Lisa, the god, had taken the yams in his sleep.

Lisa denied this, and accused Legba of his usual mischief. But when he agreed to try his own foot in the prints, it matched exactly.

The people mocked Lisa for stealing from himself, and he realized that his son had tricked him. After that the great god Lisa left the world with his wife and retreated to live in the heavens.

Legba was left on earth, but he went up to the sky every night to give an account to his father of what had gone on below during the day.

Dan Ayido Hwedo, the Divine Python

A different story says that Mawu was the supreme being, and tells how the earth was created by him and Dan Ayido Hwedo.

Dan Ayido Hwedo, the divine python or rainbow snake, was the first thing that Mawu, the great god, created. The python then carried Mawu in his mouth as they went around creating the rest of the world.

Everywhere they stopped for the night mountains were formed from the python's droppings. These contained precious minerals, which people have since discovered by excavating mines.

When Mawu had finished his journey, he realised that he and Dan Ayido Hwedo had overburdened the earth with mountains, trees and large animals. The world was starting to drown in the sea. Mawu asked Dan Ayido Hwedo to support the earth, and the divine python made himself into a coil so that the earth could rest on his back. Mostly the python manages to lie still, but occasionally he wriggles – and then the earth shakes.

In order to keep up Dan Ayido's strength, Mawu ordered the red monkeys who live in the sea to make iron bars for the python to eat. The earth has become ever more burdened by the weight of humans and their houses. If the monkeys should forget or refuse to feed the python, he will sink into the sea and the world will end.

How Oloxon created the Earth

The Yoruba people of Nigeria say that, in the beginning, the world was a vast, watery wasteland. Above the wasteland was the sky where Oloxon, Supreme Creator and God of the Sky, lived with the other deities.

Sometimes the gods climbed down the spiders' webs that hung across the void between them to visit the wasteland. Then one day the Supreme Creator summoned the great god Orishna Nla and told him to set about the task of creating firm ground. He gave Orishna Nla a snail's shell in which there was some loose earth, together with a pigeon and a hen with five toes.

The great god came down to the wasteland and tipped out the loose earth. Then he set the pigeon and the hen down on the earth, and they started to scratch and scatter the earth all around. Before long they had covered much of the marsh with the earth, and in this way solid ground was formed. Then Oloxon told Orishna Nla to plant trees, and gave him the nut of the original palm tree. Three other species of trees were also planted, and rain fell to water them and make them grow. The creation of earth took four days, and the fifth day was given to worshipping the great god.

Now that the earth was ready to receive them, the great god made human beings from clay. However, the task of bringing the clay figures to life was reserved for Oloxon, the Supreme Creator. Orishna Nla was jealous of Oloxon's ability to create life, and hid himself so that he could watch and see how it was done. But the Creator knew everything and sent him into a deep sleep. When he woke up the human beings had already come to life.

The great god still only makes the figures of men and women, and sometimes he leaves scars and marks on them as a sign of his displeasure.

The Bringers of Fire

In African mythology there are many different stories about the discovery of fire. The Pygmy hunters of Zaire, who live in the forests along the Congo River say that they were the first to obtain fire, and this is how it happened.

One day a Pygmy was chasing an elephant and found he had arrived at the village where God lived. A fire was burning, so he seized a brand and ran off with it. God caught him and took it back. This happened three times, until finally God was fed up with the Pygmy and made a liana fence all round the village to keep him out. However, the Pygmy was easily able to jump over the liana, and so he brought fire safely back to his own camp.

According to the tales of the Dogon People of Tanzania, one of their ancestors acquired fire by stealing a piece of the sun from the Nummo spirits, the heavenly blacksmiths.

The female Nummo threw a flash of lightning at the ancestor, but he protected himself with the leather bag that he had brought with him to carry the piece of sun. Then the male Nummo threw a thunderbolt, but the ancestor managed to escape by sliding down a rainbow to earth. However he fell to the ground with such a jolt that he broke both his arms and legs in two. Although he recovered, since that time all men and women have had joints at the knees and elbows.

MASON WASP

S ometimes animals are credited with the acquisition of fire.

The Ila people of Zambia say that a mason wasp brought fire from heaven. The mason wasp is one of the commonest insects in Africa. It often builds its mud nest in fireplaces, which is why the Ila associate the mason wasp with fire.

Originally there was no fire on earth, and all the birds and insects met together to discuss how they could keep warm. One of them suggested that perhaps God had fire, and the mason wasp volunteered to go and get it. The vulture, the fish eagle and the crow offered to go with him. Saying good-bye, they flew off towards heaven.

A few days later some bones fell down to the ground. They were those of the vulture. These were followed by the bones of the fish eagle, and the small bones of the crow. The mason wasp travelled on alone, resting on the clouds but never managing to reach the heavens. Eventually God took pity on the wasp and said that since he was the only one to survive the adventure he would make him head of all the birds and insects. He said that if he built his nest near the fireplace and left an egg there, when he returned in a few days he would find the egg changed into a wasp like himself. And so it has been ever since – the mason wasp always builds his mud nest near a fireplace because God told him to do so.

MANTIS

T he San Bushmen say that fire was stolen by the praying mantis, a creature that they regard as sacred.

One day Mantis noticed appetizing smells coming from the place where the ostrich was eating. He went over to investigate and saw that Ostrich was roasting food on a fire. When he had finished eating, Ostrich tucked the fire away under his wing.

Then Mantis thought of a trick by which he could get the fire for himself. He went to Ostrich and said, 'I have found a wonderful tree with delicious fruit. Follow me and I will show you.'

Ostrich followed Mantis to a tree that was covered with delicious, yellow plums. Ostrich began to eat greedily, but Mantis said, 'Reach up, the best fruit are at the top.'

Ostrich stood on tiptoe and reached up. As he opened his wings wide to balance himself, Mantis stole the fire from under them. From that time on Ostrich has never spread his wings to fly again, but has kept them close to his body.

Ol-Olin and his Rivalry with God

According to the Yoruba people of Nigeria, all the oceans, seas and rivers of the world are also inhabited by gods.

The god of the sea, Ol-Olin, lived in a magnificent underwater palace made of coral and precious stones. He was attended by a vast retinue of servants, some of whom were human, while others were fish. When he was not in his palace, Ol-Olin would ride across the ocean waves in a silver chariot drawn by exotic flying fish.

Ol-Olin was a vain and proud god who was always trying to rival the splendour of God himself. One day he decided to challenge the Supreme Creator to a contest. God was to appear in his finest clothes, and Ol-Olin would do the same. The lesser deities would judge who was the most splendidly dressed.

At the appointed time, God sent his messenger, the chameleon, to fetch Ol-Olin for the contest. When the god of the sea emerged from his ocean palace dressed in his best finery, with a necklace of shells around his neck, he was surprised to see that the messenger of God was wearing a splendid costume similar to his own. He turned back quickly, and put on even finer robes and some coral beads, but when he came out the chameleon had also changed into the same clothes.

Ol-Olin went back a third time, and clothed himself in robes studded with pearls and a golden crown. Again the chameleon appeared in a similar dress.

Seven times Ol-Olin tried to outdo the chameleon, but each time he was matched by the same costume. Finally the god of the sea gave up his challenge. If the divine messenger was so glorious, he thought, then he didn't stand a chance against God. So Ol-Olin remained in second place to the Supreme Creator, and the land triumphed over the sea.

Ifa and Eshu

Ifa was the god of wisdom, order and control according to the Yoruba people of Nigeria. He came to earth to teach the secrets of medicine and of prophecy to humans.

Eshu was a trickster god, a cunning mediator between heaven and earth. He was responsible for all the quarrels that occurred between human beings and for the arguments between humans and the gods.

I fa and Eshu travelled around together, but they often quarrelled. One day, Eshu boasted that he could easily bring ruin upon Ifa.

Ifa just laughed and said, 'If you do that, you will bring destruction to yourself as well. Heaven has ordained that we two should work together.'

That night, while Ifa was asleep, Eshu stole a cockerel from a nearby farm and cut off its head.

Hiding the body under his coat, he returned to Ifa and said, 'Wake up! Death is coming!'

In the distance, Ifa and Eshu could hear the farmer and his family approaching. They were very angry at the loss of their cockerel.

As the two gods fled, Eshu slyly sprinkled drops of blood from the dead cockerel to mark their trail. Ifa looked back and saw that the farmer was carrying an axe, so he changed himself into a bird and flew up into a tall tree.

Eshu did the same and, perching next to him, said, 'There! Didn't I tell you that I would bring ruin on you?'

'Whatever happens to me, will happen to you too,' Ifa replied.

The farmer chopped down the tree and waited for the gods to fall, but instead of dead bodies, he found only a stone and a pool of clear, cool water.

When he looked at the stone, his head filled with heat and pain. It was only when he turned and looked at the beautiful pool that the pain disappeared. The farmer recognized that a miracle had happened and bowed down to worship the gods.

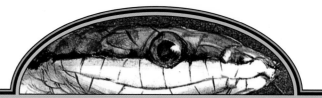

Australasia and the Pacific

Before the Aborigines lived in Australia, there was a time called the Dreamtime, when the land was occupied by the spirit ancestors of all the people, plants and animals living there today. These ancestors travelled across Australia shaping the landscape and creating natural phenomena. The idea that the actions of ancestral spirits, or gods, remain alive and effective among the living human descendants is familiar in the mythology of all parts of the Pacific.

Why the Sun goes away at Night

Worship of the sun is common throughout the Pacific. The people of New Guinea say that long ago the sun was owned by a young man who kept it in a dish. He inherited the sun from his father, a powerful god.

The young man's sister cooked food for him, but when she got married, her husband was jealous and brought him stones to eat instead of the food she had cooked. The young man decided he would go and live somewhere else.

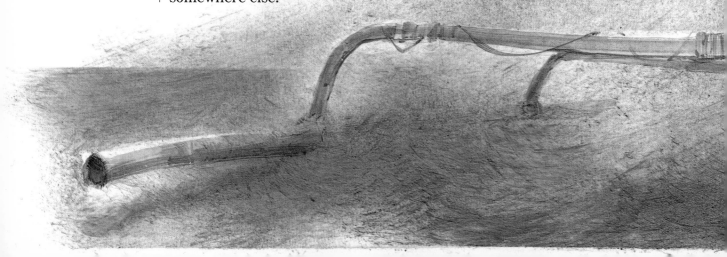

Taking the sun with him, he set off in his canoe towards the east. There he landed on a beach and fell asleep. He was woken the next morning by a group of young women, bringing food and gifts. They welcomed him and made him king of their island, because he was the only man and he brought the sunshine with him.

Meanwhile in his home village it was always night. The people found they could grow no food in the darkness, so they were soon starving to death. The young man's sister set off in search of her brother, the owner of the sun.

She travelled far and wide, and at last she saw a streak of light in the east. She finally landed on the island where her brother was king and persuaded him to come back home with her. He put the sun, which had the shape of a shining round seashell, in his boat, and together they travelled westward. The starving people soon felt better when they saw the sun rise and were able to cultivate crops again.

However the owner of the sun did not stay. He sailed away again to the island where he was king. But he promised to return every morning, and he has kept his promise to this day.

Yurlunggur, the Rainbow Serpent

Aborigines living in Arnhem Land in northern Australia tell of a great flood that they ascribe to the rainbow serpent. In the beginning this creature was responsible for digging out many of the waterholes and river beds as it writhed across Australia. Even today, the serpent sometimes rises from a waterhole and arches itself across the sky as a rainbow.

Two sisters, Waimiri and Bolaliri, lived in Wawalag country near the Roper River. One day they set off to travel to the northern coast of Arnhem Land to look for food. The elder sister carried her small son under her arm in a paper bark cradle. The younger sister was heavily pregnant. The sisters took with them their two female dogs, Wulngari and Buruwal, and they carried baskets full of stone spearheads.

The sisters travelled through many places. Along the way they collected edible plants and roots to eat. With the help of their dogs they hunted small animals – lizards, possum, bandicoots, wallabies, and goannas. They named each species of animal and plant, as well as the places through which they walked.

Then the time came for Bolaliri to give birth to her baby. The sisters set up camp beside a waterhole, not realizing that this was the home of the

▽ This story, told by the Yolngu people, explains how the monsoon came, to bring the wet season to the Pacific.

The swallowing of the Wawalag sisters and their sons is re-enacted during the initiation ceremony for adolescent Yolngu boys. Each episode of the rite, which represents a symbolic death before rebirth as an adult, is accompanied by songs which describe in detail the relevant part of the myth.

great serpent god, Yurlunggur. Waimiri collected soft bark to make a bed for her sister, and branches to make a shelter.

Bolaliri's child was born, and Waimiri washed the new-born boy at the waterhole. Some of the blood fell into the water and polluted it, and this enraged the rainbow serpent. When Waimiri tried to cook supper, she found that all the food jumped from the fire and dived into the waterhole.

'Oh, sister, something is wrong,' Waimiri wailed in despair.

'Maybe there is a snake here,' suggested Bolaliri.

But it was too dark to leave that place, and Bolaliri was tired and needed to rest after giving birth.

During the night Yurlunggur created a violent storm, with lightning, thunder and heavy rain. Torrents of water came flooding over the ground. Inside the shelter, Waimiri and Bolaliri sang sacred songs to try and calm the storm and drive the serpent away.

The storm eventually abated and the sisters thought that the serpent had gone. But he was still there,

waiting. He was singing, making them drowsy, and soon they slept.

Yurlunggur emerged from his waterhole, stretched himself, stood erect, and then lowered himself again. He put his head into the shelter and wrapped his body round and round it, as a python does with his prey. Then he swallowed them all – the sisters, the dogs, their small sons and the baskets of stone spears – in one enormous bite.

The rainbow serpent rose up to the sky and all the other serpent gods rose there, too, from their waterholes. Each serpent told what he had eaten. Yurlunggur boasted about his meal, but just then an ant bit him and he vomited up the sisters, dogs, babies and stone spears.

The serpent swallowed the sisters again, but this time he left the male children, who became the first Yolngu initiates. The sisters lost to the snake the creatures they had named and their ritual songs as well.

Two men, who had heard the storm, came to see what was happening. After learning the songs which the sisters had sung, they carried out the first Yolngu initiation ceremony.

Ranginui and Papa

anginui the sky god and his wife Papa, the earth goddess, were united in an eternal embrace. All their many children, except for Tawhiri, the god of the winds, decided it would be a good idea to separate their parents because it was dark on earth and there was no room for any creatures to grow, to walk or to fly.

Tumatauenga, the god of war, suggested that they should kill their parents, and separate them that way. But the other gods and goddesses were horrified at this idea and refused to agree to it.

The forced separation was finally achieved by Tane, god of the forest and of light, who assumed the form of a tree and forced the sky upwards. He then covered his father's naked body with Ika-Roa, the Milky Way, and his mother's body he carpeted with forests, ferns and other plants.

The sky god complained at the separation from his beloved wife and wept tears of rain. But Tane replied that their descendants needed light in order to live and grow.

Light then became visible on earth and many creatures appeared that had been hidden by the parents' bodies. Reptiles, mammals, and even the first human beings rose up and stood blinking in the new light.

However Tawhiri's anger at the sorrow of his parents led to a war between the gods, which resulted in storms that tore up Tane's forests and tidal waves that disturbed Tangaroa's fishes and reptiles in the sea. Many reptiles fled from the sea into the forest, and Tangaroa quarrelled with Tane for letting them in.

Tane got his revenge by showing his brother, Tu-of-the-Angry-Face, how to make canoes, nets, spears, and fish hooks from the forest plants, so that he might catch the fishes of Tangaroa.

▽ This story of how the Earth was made is told on many of the islands of Polynesia (the southeastern group of islands in the Pacific Ocean, running eastwards from Tonga and Samoa).

TANGAROA AND RONGO

Tangaroa and Rongo are said to be the twin sons of Ranginui and Papa. Tangaroa is the god of the oceans and breathes only twice in twenty-four hours – which we know as the tides. Rongo is god of all cultivated foods, especially of sweet potatoes.

Tangaroa should have been the first-born son, but he gave precedence to his brother and emerged, a few days later, from a boil on his mother's arm. As the rightful first-born son, Ranginui wanted to make Tangaroa sole heir to all his parents' property.

However Papa thought it would be better to distribute their possessions between the two. All things that were reddish in colour became Tangaroa's, and everything else went to Rongo.

Tangaroa's red food was more colourful, but Rongo had much more. This did not please Tangaroa, so he set off in a canoe loaded with his red foods and visited many islands until he finally settled in Rarotonga and Aitutaki.

TU-OF-THE-ANGRY-FACE

As time went by all the sons of Ranginui and Papa quarrelled with each other, but Tu-of-the-Angry-Face outwitted them all. With Tane's help, he made traps for the animals of the forest and sails to capture the

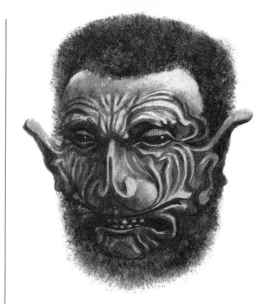

wind. He ate the children of Rongo, the god of cultivated foods, and pulled up the children of Haumia, the god of foods that grew wild.

IRI AND RINGGON

Some say that two birds, Iri and Ringgon, created the world. When they had made all the plants and animals, they decided to make human beings. First they made a figure out of clay, but it could not move. Then they carved a figure from hard wood, but it could not speak.

After much thought, the birds then took some wood from the Kumpong tree, which has very strong fibres and bright red sap. From this they made a perfect man and woman. The birds were delighted with these models, and spent a long time admiring them.

However, when they tried to make some more just like them, they found that they had forgotten the design. Further efforts to repeat their success produced very poor models, and these, it is said, became the ancestors of the apes.

△ Tangaroa created many of the islands in the western Pacific at the request of his messenger bird, Tula, who wanted somewhere to rest.

When Tula complained there was no shade, Tangaroa planted a vine for him, but as it grew it sprouted men and women instead of leaves. That is how, it is said, those islands were first populated.

How Batara Guru made the Earth

The islands of Indonesia have many different stories about how the world was created by the great god, Batara Guru.

One story tells how the god's wife, who was expecting a baby, longed for venison to eat. Batara Guru sent a raven to find some. He roamed around the heavens without success, and eventually came to a cave that contained a deep pit.

The raven threw a bamboo cane down to see just how deep it was, and then flew down into the seemingly bottomless pit. He emerged on the surface of a dark sea, but only then did he realize that he could not find his way back. Fortunately the cane floated by, so he could perch on it and rest.

Meanwhile Batara Guru, accompanied by several servants, set out from the heavens to look for the raven. He took with him a handful of soil, seven pieces of wood, a chisel, a goat and a bumble bee. Batara Guru arrived at the dark sea and was beginning to make a raft with the pieces of wood when the raven floated up on the bamboo cane. He asked Batara Guru to throw some light on the scene, which the god did.

Then Batara Guru told the goat to get down under the raft and steady it on his horns. The goat, accompanied by the bumble bee, did this, but just at that moment the god broke his chisel. The broken piece flew from his hand and hit the goat hard on the head.

The goat bucked wildly, so that the raft was badly shaken. Batara Guru ordered the goat to keep still, and then spread his handful of soil over the raft. Thus he made the earth, and gave it to the raven for his home.

In another story, Batara Guru's daughter, Boru Deak Pordjar, was trying to escape from the unwanted attentions of her uncle, and leapt from the heavens into the bottomless pit of the sea.

Batara Guru sent a swallow to her with a handful of soil, which she scattered on the sea to make the earth. The earth shut out all the light from the underworld kingdom of the great serpent Naga Padoha. This made him very angry, so he rose up and drowned the earth. Batara Guru fixed Naga Padoha to a rock, and recreated the earth above the serpent's head. People say that one day he may break free and destroy the earth in one huge quake.

▽ There are ten large and other 3,000 small islands in the various island groups that make up Indonesia.

On the island of Sumatra, it is always said that the great god, Batara Guru, made the Earth out of a handful of soil.

There are hundreds of books about the gods and goddesses of the world and their doings. Go and look in your local library or your nearest bookshop and you will find a good choice of books to investigate. The following list includes some classic versions that you should look out for and some books for adults which you might find interesting.

A good collection of myths and legends from around the world can be found in the Oxford University Press's (OUP) series: OXFORD MYTHS & LEGENDS.

Children's books that will tell you more

Central and South American Stories, Robert Hull (Wayland).

Coyote makes Man, James Sage (SoftbABCks).

Folktales and Fables of the Americas and the Pacific, Mollie Perham and Robert Ingpen (Dragon's World).

Folktales and Fables of Asia and Australia, Mollie Perham and Robert Ingpen (Dragon's World).

Folktales and Fables of Europe, Mollie Perham and Robert Ingpen (Dragon's World).

Folktales and Fables of the Middle East and Africa, Mollie Perham and Robert Ingpen (Dragon's World).

MYSTERIOUS PLACES series:
The Lands of the Bible, The Mediterranean, Robert Ingpen and Jacqueline Dineen; *The Master Builders, The Magical East*, Robert Ingpen and Michael Pollard (Dragon's World): this series will tell you a lot about the various peoples who worshipped the gods and goddesses described in this book and where and what their holy places were.

Myths of the Norsemen, Roger Lancelyn Green (Puffin).

Tales of Ancient Egypt, Roger Lancelyn Green (Puffin).

Adult books you might enjoy

Aboriginal Mythology, Nyoongah (Aquarian Press).

Dragons, Gods & Spirits from Chinese Mythology, Tao Tao Liu Saunders (Peter Lowe).

Encyclopedia of Gods, Michael Jordan (Kyle Cathie): this book lists the gods and goddesses by name.

Encyclopedia of Things That Never Were, Michael Page and Robert Ingpen (Dragon's World).

Gods, Demons and Others, R.K. Narayan (Mandarin).

A Guide to the Gods, Richard Carlyon (Heinemann, Quixote Press): this book lists the gods and goddesses by area.

Kings, Gods & Spirits from African Mythology, Jan Knappert (Peter Lowe).

The Mahabarata, R.K. Narayan (Mandarin).

Mesopotamian Myths (British Museum Publications): this includes myths of the Assyrians, Babylonians and Sumerians.

Monkey, Wu Ch'êng-ên (Penguin).

Myths and Legends of China, E.T.C. Werner (Dover Publications).

Myths and Legends of Japan, F. Hadland Davis (Dover Publications).

Pears Encyclopedia of Myths and Legends [in four volumes], Mary Barker & Christopher Cook (editors) (Pelham).

The Ramayana, R.K. Narayan (Vision Press).

Roman Myths, Michael Grant (Penguin).

Spirits, Heroes & Hunters from North American Indian Mythology, Marion Wood (Peter Lowe).

Warriors, Gods & Spirits from Central & South American Mythology, Douglas Gifford (Peter Lowe).